# Hobie Hanson, You're Weird

So I started first. I smooshed my head back and forth across the pie, ate two gigantic bites, and then raised up so she could take over. It wasn't bad. A little pasty, but not bad.

Molly carefully lowered her head and stuck her tongue out a little toward the cream at the edge of the crust. She'd said she wouldn't bite me, and she didn't, but she wasn't biting the pie either! I couldn't believe it! If I was going to risk permanent embarrassment by eating a coconut cream pie with Molly Bosco, I was at least going to win some kind of prize for it.

So I put my hand very gently on the back of her head and shoved her face into the pie as hard as I could.

# Hobie Hanson, YOU'RE WEIRD

## by Jamie Gilson

### Illustrations by Elise Primavera

A Beech Tree Paperback Book
New York

## To Anne,
### who is wry, wonderful, and—well—weird

The Library of Congress has cataloged the Lothrop, Lee & Shepard Books
edition of *Hobie Hanson, You're Weird* as follows:
Gilson, Jamie. Hobie Hanson, you're weird.
Summary: With his best friend away at computer camp, Hobie reluctantly shares adventures with a girl classmate the summer after fourth grade.  ISBN 0-688-06700-X
I. Primavera, Elise, ill.  II. Title.  PZ7.G4385Ho 1987 [Fic] 86-15241

5 7 9 10 8 6 4
First Beech Tree Edition, 1996
ISBN 0-688-14747-X

# Contents

# 1

# Good-for-Nothing Kid

"Jingle bells, Batman smells,
 Robin laid an egg.
 The Batmobile lost a wheel and . . .

Um, um, um-um-um," Toby hummed. "What comes next?" he asked us. Toby is Nick Rossi's four-year-old brother, and he asks a lot of questions. Nick and I didn't answer.

A lot of times we don't answer. This time we weren't about to because we'd just stomped out of Nick's house, mad. Toby had stomped after us, hugging his new green-and-white-striped beach ball with yellow stars on it.

" 'Jingle bells, Batman smells . . .' " he started again, aiming the ball at Nick's head.

"I won't go!" Nick yelled at the house. "You can't make me," he told his dad, who couldn't hear him. Catching the ball before it punched his nose, he drop-kicked it with a blast so hard it cleared the chimney. I was impressed. Being mad sometimes makes you strong, but I was impressed, anyway.

Toby watched the ball fly and ran to fetch it.

"If you don't want to go, get your dad to send me instead," I told Nick. I mean, I went to camp once for two nights and I didn't die, so I could just go and suffer in his place. What are friends for? Nick and I have lived next door to each other practically always, since all we did was drool and chew on the tails of rubber ducks. Almost ten years. "Hey, it sounds like a barrel of monkeys to me."

"Barrel of monkeys! More like a sack of skunks. Did you *see* this stuff about Mighty Byte Camp?" He waved the folder at me. "I mean, computers, math, and weight lifting for *six weeks*! That's sick. It's also practically the whole summer."

"Not just weight lifting. They've got canoes, too," I said, trying to cheer him up.

"Sure, and you know what else?" Flapping the folder open, he read, " 'Cindy says she loved programming her P.C. and then paddling on our lovely lagoon. Cindy says Mighty Byte was the most fun time she's ever had!' " He tossed the folder into the bushes. "What else they've got—is girls."

"Yuck," I agreed.

"Yuck," Toby said behind us. "The ball's stuck, Nick. You got to get it down."

Nick ignored him. "Besides, you and I were going to mow lawns and coin a bundle this summer." His shoulders sagged. He shook his head like he knew he was sunk, like he knew he'd be marooned in a canoe with Cindy every sweaty afternoon after five hours of inputting pre-algebra. "You know, I think my dad is practically bonkers, sending me off to a prison like Mighty Byte. Maybe he should see a shrink."

"*Your* dad should see a shrink? What about mine? He gets these crazy ideas, like I'm a science experiment."

Toby started to yowl. He does that sometimes when we don't listen to him. His yowl isn't as bad as his bite, though, so we went with him to find out where the ball had landed.

The windows were open because it was June and sunny and warm, so we could still hear the argument going on inside Nick's house. His dad and my dad were having it out. They're good friends like Nick and me, but you'd never know it when they talk about summer and kids. We'd heard it all before, with different words, but we listened anyway, thinking maybe this time the fight would end up happy.

"Roger, you are a dinosaur," Nick's dad told my dad. "You are mired in the past."

"Yeah," I said to Nick. "A dinosaur."

"Listen, I happen to know what's right for my son. *You* are making a *robot* out of your kid." My dad boomed so loud, the blue jays flapped off the big bird feeder that looks like Saturn. "We have to let kids have a *childhood*!" he yelled as the birds flew.

See, my dad has this theory that kids don't have time to be kids anymore because they're programmed by their parents and teachers to *do* stuff all the time. So what he wanted me to do all summer was—nothing!

"Orders. I personally am sick of taking orders," he'd tell me. "They yell, 'Roger, send the tow truck. Roger, fix the bashed fender. Roger, make this wreck look like it just drove out of the showroom. Roger, do it now!' Listen, I wish *I* could just fool around like Tom Sawyer. You and I could do some things together. Go backpacking over a long weekend. Your mother, too. What d'you think? I wish *I* was nine years old." Then he'd sigh, a long, deep sigh.

"I'm almost ten," I'd tell him, but he wouldn't listen.

Anyway, I wasn't sure how to fool around like Tom Sawyer. So I checked the book out. I even made a list.

### Things Tom Sawyer did:
√ Caught flies
√ Went fishing
√ Flung dead cats in graveyards

√ Skipped school
√ Conned some kids into whitewashing a fence
√ Kissed a girl on purpose
√ Found a sack of gold worth $12,000
√ Lifted his teacher's wig with a cat's claws on the last day of school.

Now, some of that sounded pretty good to me, but Mr. Star, our teacher, doesn't wear a wig. Also, I don't come across a lot of dead cats. I'd gone to a graveyard at midnight once, but it wasn't much fun. Catching flies is OK. So is fishing, but not every day. As for kissing a girl on purpose, the people on TV clearly like it, but it seems dumb to me.

Somehow, the summer Dad and Mom had in mind for me didn't sound like dead cats and gold. And I wasn't exactly going to be doing nothing, either. Dad would leave for work at seven, Mom at eight. I'd have to do the dishes and stuff and clean the cat's box. Then I was supposed to go next door and baby-sit Toby until noon, see he didn't chase any balls into the street or eat dirt, and teach him his 1, 2, 3s and ABCs so he'd be ready for prekindergarten in the fall. Mrs. Rossi would feed me bologna-and-cheese sandwiches and let me out at one o'clock to be Tom Sawyer until Mom got home at four-thirty. Big deal.

"He'll be free as a bird," my dad shouted at Nick's dad and the whole neighborhood.

It didn't seem worth listening to any more. This was a song we knew. Besides, Toby had stopped yelling about the stuck ball and started baring his baby fangs. Sure enough, the ball was on the roof, snagged in a bend of the gutter.

"Let's try sticks," Nick said, and he heaved one. It stuck behind the ball. We threw another and another, about a million all together, but the ball held them all fast. It looked like we were building a nest, like maybe some gigantic green-and-white bird with yellow stars on it might settle down and hatch the thing. The twigs Toby threw, though, were making a nest at his toes.

"OK," Nick told him, "I'll go get it, but this is absolutely the last time I do," like he wasn't the one who kicked the ball there in the first place.

Nick climbed the tree next to the house, shinnied across a branch, and leaped to the roof. He flung himself flat on the shingles, then turned and sat swinging his legs from side to side. He lifted the ball from its nest and tucked it under his arm.

"Give it!" Toby called. Nick twirled the ball on his finger so the stars spun, and then flicked it into the yard.

"Computers are the future!" Nick's dad was taking his turn. "My Nick will be ready. If your kid does nothing, that's what he'll be good for. Nothing. A good-for-nothing Tom Sawyer kid!" I thought that was a little strong.

My dad must have thought so too, because we heard the front door slam behind him and watched as he stormed down the sidewalk.

After that we waited awhile, listening to the quiet and watching the blue jays fly back again to peck up seed in the feeder.

"If I stay up here, they can't send me to Mighty Byte," Nick said, finally.

"They'll starve you down. Or pick you off with a crane." I scratched my back against the tree trunk.

Nick stood up on the tilting shingles just above the gutter and started to belt out, " 'Jingle bells, Batman smells,' " so you knew right away where Toby had learned it. " 'Robin laid an egg. The Batmobile lost a wheel . . .' " Flapping his arms in the air, he stretched up. " 'The Batmobile lost a wheel' . . . And I can't go to Mighty Byte . . ." he sang, ". . . if I break my . . ."

"Don't *do* it!" I yelled. Toby grabbed my shirt, staring up at Nick, and yowled.

Nick gave a whoop, flapped some more, and grinned so all his teeth showed. Then, raising his arms high, he flung himself through the air like he had on a cape and was Batman, Robin, and more. Toby watched him head for the ground and shrieked.

On TV once I heard one of those Super Guys talking, his head almost sticking out of the screen, he was so sincere. "Now, boys and girls," he said, as sweet as candy corn, "don't *you* try to fly. You might cause yourself permanent bodily harm. You've got to leave super stunts like that to Super Me," or something like that. But kids aren't that dumb.

Even Nick. It wasn't all that far from roof to grass. We'd both jumped it before. Your teeth jiggle a little when you crash, and your nose feels like somebody has salted it from the inside, but you don't die or anything. Nick's bones hardly bent. He cheated, anyway, catching on to a branch and swinging partway down. Still, it's the thought that counts. He did tilt forward and mash his nose a little. Whenever Nick smashes his nose, it bleeds. This time it bled like a waterfall.

Toby saw the red flood and cried like fanged bats had got him. I yelled, too, just to help out. Nick gave a weak beep. The blue jays cawed. We were a very good chorus.

But not good enough. Nose blood and screams wouldn't help. Fourth grade was shot. There were only two days left. After Friday everybody else would be packing shorts and planning big summer stuff. Then Nick would be off with boats and bytes and girls. And here I'd be, a good-for-nothing Tom Sawyer without a Huckleberry Finn.

# 2

## Thrills, Chills, and Smells

"OK, kids," Mr. Star said. "I want to see you treat this Thursday like any other Thursday." On the chalkboard behind him somebody had written, "I ♡ Mr. Star." The periods were hearts, too. "Vacation doesn't start till tomorrow afternoon," he warned us. "So keep it down to a low, mild roar."

The roar was high in 4B, but it wasn't wild. I mean, we weren't flat-dropping books or burping do-re-mi. We were talking. Mr. Star had told us to talk. We had to interview each other for our last Language Arts assignment. And he'd said we could sit anywhere so long as we behaved, so that's where most people were sitting. Anywhere.

Nick, who had to interview Lisa Soloman, had headed for his favorite Anywhere place. He lay on his belly under the big table in the back of the room, his elbows sunk in a Cubs cushion with foam rubber bulging out its seams. His feet were hooked over the bar of the closest chair. Lisa sat under the far corner of the table, propped against a leg. Even in the dark under there I could see the glowing green ME on her T-shirt and her green lightning-bolt earrings with pink Day-Glo blobs on the ends. "This is, like, too much," she told him.

A couple of kids had climbed up on the counter next to the sink. Two were on the ledge in front of the windows, notebooks in their laps, their feet dangling over the cold radiators. Others just sat cross-legged on the floor.

I was at my desk like regular, because I was stuck interviewing with Molly Bosco, boss of the world, who sat right in front of me. She had a huge pink clip that looked like a killer butterfly in her brown hair. In her hand she held a new pencil with gold lettering that read "Central School Is Number One. Learn a Lot and Have Some Fun." It was so sharp she could have given flu shots with it. One whole page of her spiral notebook was filled with questions and one-line spaces for answers. Molly was always prepared.

"Name?" She checked off question one.

I groaned. "Come on, Bosco, you've known me since first grade. After four years you still don't know my name?"

She smiled and waited.

I waited too, without smiling, but that was getting us nowhere. So I gave in. "Hobie Hanson."

She started writing and then erased it. "Hobie isn't your real name. It's *Hobart*."

"It is not," I lied, and she rolled her eyes. She knew I was lying, because when we were in second grade all the kids called me Hobarf, or sometimes just Barfy, for short. "OK, but when I get old enough, I'm going to change it. H-O-B-A-R-T Hanson." I gave her the old evil eye, daring her to make something of it.

Molly flipped her long dark hair with the eraser end of the pencil. "What's your favorite color, *Hobart?*" I crossed my arms and my eyes, and she sighed with this huge rush of air that must have half collapsed her lungs. "Oh, come on, Hobie, everybody's got a favorite color. I made this list especially easy, so you'd know at least *some* of the answers."

Nothing is more boring than somebody's favorite color. Unless it's their favorite number or day of the week. I shook my head sadly to let her know how dull it was. "That's a dumb, stupid question," I said, as nice as I could. Mr. Star had talked to us and talked to us before we started about being polite and helpful to the people interviewing us. So I was. "I have never heard a dumber, stupider question," I explained politely.

"I'll put down 'color blind.' " She blinked her eyes at Mr. Star, who was watching us, and then dotted the *i* with a little heart.

"OK, gray," I answered. "The color of sharks and toenails."

She didn't gag like she was supposed to, I'll give her that. Instead she heaved another major sigh and wrote, in her big, round, even handwriting, "Gray."

"OK, favorite food?"

"Cold Cream of Wheat with black bug sprinkles," I said.

She rapped the desk with her pencil, getting mad but not sick. "Cereal," she wrote.

"Come on," I told her, "ask me *good* stuff. Ask me my favorite joke, or which comic-strip character I want to be, or what's buried in the bottom of my dresser drawer." That's what I was going to ask her.

She sighed again, louder than most people talk. "Thank you so much for your advice, HO-bart, but those are *really* stupid questions. What is your favorite number?"

"Thirteen," I said, and smiled.

She stuck out her tongue. Behind us I could hear Nick's voice echo out from under the table. He was telling Lisa that his pet peeve was Hobie Hanson. When I turned around to shove the chair his feet were hanging on to, he pulled himself back like a turtle. Molly kicked at me, but I dodged her.

Mr. Star advanced on us. "I see some behavior that's inappropriate," he said.

"When's your birthday?" Molly went on, smiling up sweetly at Mr. Star.

"July Fourth," I told her. "That's why I wear my hair in bangs. Get it? Fourth of July. Firecrackers. Booms. Bangs!"

"Hobie Hanson, you're weird," she said.

"Look, weird is just *different*," I explained. "What's wrong with that?"

She shrugged. "OK, so what are you going to do this summer?"

She *would* ask that question. All around us kids were answering it. David was going to hockey camp. Rolf was spending the summer with his father in Utah. R.X. was pitcher of his Little League team, and they stuck together. Eugene and his parents were going to Korea to visit his family there. And I'd seen Marshall and Trevor's poster up in Meat 'n' Shoppe, saying the Mar-Vor Marvels would mow lawns and wash windows. It had a border of smiley faces and a strip of tear-off phone numbers. Action-packed, fun-filled, four-star summers.

Molly tapped her eraser on her desk.

I chewed the insides of my cheeks. I had to think of something weirder still. "Catch flies," I told her, laughing like that was pretty wacky. "Tom Sawyer did it, and he had great summers. My dad says."

She didn't laugh back. She just cocked her head

and narrowed her eyes. "Catch flies," she wrote. "OK, favorite day of the week?"

"That's really creative! Wow, day of the week! That needs an especially creative answer. Golly, Molly, how about Monday, because that's when I get to see *you* after the long dull weekend."

She kicked me under the chair, catching the edge of my kneecap. Inappropriate behavior. Besides, it hurt.

"Gargling with Scope every morning," Nick answered behind me, but I didn't catch the question.

"Girlfriend's name?" Molly asked.

I rubbed my knee and nodded to Mr. Star as he passed. I thought about ratting on Molly and rolling up my pants to show him the inappropriate big black bruise, but it wasn't worth it.

"Girlfriend?" she asked again, pencil ready.

"Molly Bosco," I told her, pushing my nose up into a snout. "She's a real sweetheart."

She stuck her finger in her mouth and aarged, but wrote it down anyway.

"OK, time to change sides," Mr. Star announced, and it was my turn to question.

Molly was all set to answer favorite animal and TV show, but I didn't ask those. When I asked comic-strip character, she knew right away that she'd be Brenda Starr, because then, she said, her name would be practically like Mr. Star's. Her favorite joke was a real howler: "What is black and white, black and white, black and white and green? Three skunks fighting over a pickle." In the bottom of her dresser she's got this pink net bag filled with orange peels, peach pits, and cloves that she made in Girl Scouts. Not bad. Not as good as my bottom drawer, though. It's filled with excellent junk—date-nut cookie fossils, green glass and sand from the beach, armless monsters, a wind-up snail, and best of all, a blue plastic soap box with practically my complete set of baby teeth in it. They were returned one night by the tooth fairy, who must have had an overstock. I've stuck them all in Silly Putty so they look like little-kid false teeth.

"Unicorn puffy stickers," I heard Lisa tell Nick.

"You're kidding," he said. "Why? OK, OK. Best friend?"

"Molly Bosco," she said, loud enough for Molly to hear. I bet Jenny, Michelle, and most of the rest of the girls said it loud too.

"Now make these good, clear, neatly written paragraphs," Mr. Star called out. "Something quite special is going to happen to them."

Right, I thought. I'm getting an A for asking awesome questions. Molly's getting a D for asking dull ones. I still had a couple of lines left on the page.

"Ask me what *I'm* going to do this summer." Molly lifted her chin and smiled like there was some guy behind me with a camera.

She was going to do something terrific. I knew it. Everybody was but me. "OK, I bite. What?"

"A contest," she said, raising her voice like she was talking to the kids across the hall in 4A. "We expect it to keep me busy all summer long. My grandmother entered my name. *I* didn't do it." She shook her head hard as if I'd said she was cheating. "My grandmother did. I wouldn't even have *thought* of it. I got this letter, see, that said I should be a local contestant in this nationwide soon-to-be-televised pageant. My parents are going to Pakistan this summer, and my grandmother was looking for something wonderful for me to do. And this is it." She took a deep breath and smiled, like I'd told her that I, personally, would give her a big blue ribbon.

"You're kidding," I said. "What kind of pageant?"

"When I win here, I get hundreds of dollars' worth of valuable merchandise, a float of my own in the Fourth of July parade, and more, much more. When I win the state and national contests, I get much, *much* more."

I cracked the tip off my pencil and stopped writing.

"The letter said somebody had sent them my name. My piano teacher, it said, or some other highly respected member of the community. I can't figure out who it was. I don't take piano, but my grandmother says that everyone knows I'm gifted and talented. She sent the pageant people a check and last year's school picture. This year's made me look like an owl."

"I bet they got your name off some list." It didn't matter that she was dying to tell me. I wanted to know. "*What* pageant people?"

"The Miss Pre-Teen Personality Pageant," she said, slow and holy, looking up at the ceiling tiles, away from ordinary me.

"Did Lisa get a letter too?" Lisa and Nick weren't interviewing each other anymore. They'd crawled out of their hole, gone back to their desks, and started making up paragraphs.

"Are you writing this down?"

"No, I just wondered. Lisa's got tons of pre-teen personality." I laughed as I said it, but Molly didn't.

"Well, yes, she did get a letter, and so did Michelle and *maybe* a couple of other girls, but they won't enter. *I'm* entering. For the talent part I'll sing something original. My grandmother says it always pays to be original."

"*Really* original, like favorite colors and numbers?" I asked her, but she didn't laugh at that either.

"Sometimes you're not as dumb as you act," she said, scribbling something on the back page of her notebook. "My personal favorites," she said, like she was making an announcement. Then she stared at my broken pencil. "Aren't you writing down about the hundreds of dollars' worth of valuable merchandise?"

The whole thing sounded phony to me. Like the stuff they warn you against on the six-o'clock news. "Why did your grandmother send a check?"

"These things cost money." She looked at me like I had Pop Rocks for brains.

"All right, group. Get those pencils moving." Mr. Star was going at us like a cheerleader. "I want color, details—lots of details, excitement. Good stuff, I want. These should not be ordinary paragraphs."

And so I wrote, using Brenda Starr, Miss Pre-Teen P., skunks, pickles, and dried orange peels. I put together an action-packed paragraph that was thrills, chills, and smells. Molly sounded like she'd been interviewed for *Lifestyles of the Rich and Famous*. It looked a little messy, of course, but then you can't have everything.

"Does neatness count?" I asked Mr. Star as he cruised by.

"Neatness always counts, but this time you won't

be getting a grade. You are writing for quite a special project."

He tucked my page into the folder he was carrying and marched to the front of the room, just as the bell rang for recess.

# 3

# Abraham Lincoln, Babe Ruth, and Me

"All right, class," Mr. Star said, waving our interview papers over his head, "we're going to bury these."

A few kids laughed. I didn't. I mean, by the time recess was over, he'd already marked them up with red pencil. Then he'd made us do them over right away in ink, with penciled-in margins so they'd look straight on the page. Miss Pre-Teen Pickle in ballpoint pen. Fifteen minutes to bell time and he tells us he's going to trash them. It wasn't fair.

"Mine stinks," Nick whispered to me. "Burying's the best thing you could do to it. Mostly it's about Lisa's collection of smelly stickers."

A lot of kids grumbled. The more they thought about it, I guess, the more they didn't want Mr. Star to toss out something they'd written in ink without even giving it a grade.

"Can I have mine back, Mr. Star?" Marshall asked. "That's the neatest stuff I ever wrote. Michelle told me all about how her gerbils keep having more gerbils and how they chew each other's tails off. I was thinking about turning it into a TV miniseries. Sex and violence."

Mr. Star grinned. "This is going to be much bigger than a miniseries, Marshall. This is going to be . . . history."

"Like Abraham Lincoln?" Michelle asked him. "Like fourscore and seven years ago? Did we really write that good?" She didn't look surprised.

Mr. Star shook his head. "Not that kind of history. That's the history of leaders, kings, presidents." He waved his hand back and forth like he was wiping that stuff out. "This history tells what the *times* were like, what ordinary people were eating, wearing, thinking." His voice rose. He really liked whatever he was talking about. "You see what I mean?"

"Like Babe Ruth is history," Molly said, letting him know that at least *she* knew what he meant. "He wore baseball uniforms and thought about hitting home runs. And he ate a lot and got fat. I saw a documentary once on TV."

Something was wrong. Mr. Star was sometimes strange, but hardly ever *this* strange. "I thought you said you were going to bury the stuff we wrote," I said. "If you want people to read about us ordinary kids, wouldn't it be a whole lot easier just to put our interviews in a folder someplace?"

He looked full of mystery. "I guess I should tell you what this is all about. I didn't before because I wanted you to write naturally." Sitting on the edge of his desk, he leaned toward us, cleared his throat, and waited for total quiet. It was the kind of quiet that makes you nervous, like maybe he was going to say that every kid in class had to go back and take second grade over again.

Marshall crossed his legs and pulled open the Velcro on his shoe. *Scritch.* Ripping Velcro calms you down, gives your fingers something to do. *Scratch.* He shut it. *Scritch. Scratch.* It seemed like a good idea, so I did mine. *Rip, catch.* Funny how that stuff never wears out the way paste would, or tape. I crossed my leg and did the other shoe. *Rip, catch, rip. Scritch, scratch, scritch.* A lot of kids were doing it now. We were a 4B of crickets.

"Silence!" Mr. Star yelled. "I don't need background music. Will you kindly stop peeling your shoes! We are talking here about your place in history!" The *rip-scratch*es stopped at once. Both my shoe flaps were open.

"The Junior Chamber of Commerce," Mr. Star went on, looking grim, "decided at their Monday-night meeting to create a Stockton time capsule.

They're going to fill it with things that show what our town is like and bury it on the anniversary of Stockton's founding. And listen to this. The capsule won't be opened until Stockton's two hundredth birthday, July tenth, 2091!" He stood up and looked us over to make sure we got the big idea. I closed the flap on one shoe and waited. "Each school is adding something. And your interviews are going into that capsule. They will be history to the people who read them, as sure as the Pilgrims are history to you. *You* will be their forefathers. What do you think of that?"

My loose shoe fell off. I thought it was awful. "You mean the only thing those people in 2091 will know about me is what *Molly* wrote?" Summer plans: catch flies. Favorite color: gray. Favorite girl: Molly Bosco. They wouldn't even know that when I said it, I was crossing my eyes and making a snout nose.

"Can I add a smelly sticker to mine?" Lisa asked, jumping out of her chair. "By then it'll probably be worth, like, a million dollars."

"Terrific!" Mr. Star said, and she tore this fat, pink-iced doughnut off a sheet of stickers. A lot of kids groaned. Smelly stickers are stupid.

"You want those people from Mars to think we stink?" Marshall asked.

"They won't be from Mars. They'll live in Stockton, probably, just as you do," Mr. Star explained patiently. "I think the sticker's a nice touch. Besides, the smell should be almost gone by then. All right." He clapped his hands together. "Now, I need a volunteer. Someone," he went on, ignoring the low moans, "who'll be in town this summer and free to attend the dedication ceremony, Wednesday, July tenth."

Kids all around me looked smug. This was one assignment no one had to do. Mr. Star wouldn't be our teacher after tomorrow. Besides, by July tenth almost everybody would be weaving baskets by the shores of lovely Lake Chiggerswamp.

"Oh, my summer is full every single minute," Molly said with a sigh. I knew she was thinking about ruby crowns, and zillions of dollars' worth of presents tied with fat red ribbons, and people calling her "Your Awesome Miss Pre-Teen Majesty."

"I need," Mr. Star said urgently, "someone to represent us, someone to add our little bit of history to—"

I stuck my hand up. Nobody else was going to. Besides, maybe I could subtract my little bit of history from the envelope when nobody was watching.

"You'll be free on July tenth, Hobie?" Mr. Star asked.

"I'll fit it in." I shrugged my shoulders. Now if

anybody said, "So what you doing this summer?"
I could always tell them I was making history. Or
burying the past.

"Well, that's that!" Mr. Star eased the papers
into a big manila envelope. Then, wouldn't you
know, he licked the flap with a big, wet, sticky
lick and sealed it tight. "Mr. Star's 4B Class, Central School," he printed, and held it high for us all
to see. "We'll send this over to City Hall with your
name clipped to it, Hobie. They'll be in touch with
you."

Behind me, Lisa giggled, and said, "Who'd want
to touch *him?*" Molly turned to her and laughed.

Mr. Star cleared his throat and started to count,
"One . . . two . . ." and the room got pin-dropping
quiet. "This morning," he went on, "Mr. Kemp's
kindergartners are making a collage for the capsule,
lots of magazine clippings that will show the children of 2091 pictures of what we ate, drank,
wore . . ."

The lunch bell rang, and we all escaped to the
cafeteria, where we ate spaghetti and bananas, drank
not-cold milk, and wore what we'd left home in
that morning.

After lunch Mr. Star started us out doing what
he called the nitty-gritty end-of-the-year stuff.
"People," he said, "tomorrow, for the last day of

school, I want you to bring as many big brown grocery bags with you as you need to carry home your desk and locker belongings. Tomorrow is Final Cleanup Day."

Sliding all the way down in my seat, I studied my deep cave of desk stuff. A lot of loose papers hung around the front—Now&Later candy wrappers; a note from Lisa to Molly, saying that Michelle didn't like David anymore, which I'd found on the floor; and a spelling test wrapped around a wad of still oozish blue bubble gum.

My desk was my friend. Since September it had taken all kinds of junk from me and never handed any of it back. Still, I didn't want to stick my hand in too far. Something just might snap at me.

The room was steamy. Summer had already started blowing in the windows.

"Today," Mr. Star went on, "I'm handing back some of your old papers and projects that I know you'll want to keep. Here, from October, are your time lines." I'd almost forgotten making time lines, October was so long ago. Mr. Star picked up one of them and flipped out a stack of four three-by-five cards pasted on a piece of thick yellow yarn about a yard long. Each card was supposed to have a story on it about an important thing that had happened to us. "This one is Nick's," Mr. Star declared, holding the yarn high and smiling like he thought it was pretty cute. "This is your life, Nick Rossi."

Nick put his forehead on the edge of the desk and covered his head with his arms.

" 'When I was five,' " Mr. Star read from one of the cards, " 'I got a new brother, but he couldn't come home because I had chicken pox.' " Nick groaned.

" 'The day they finally brought him home,' " Mr. Star read on, " 'I covered my belly with pink marker dots, redder than the chicken pox, but my mom said the hospital had a no-returns policy.' "

Nick stood up. "Mr. Star, if you read any more, I'm jumping." He held his nose and raised his hand like he was about to throw himself off the high board.

Mr. Star handed Nick his string of cards. "I almost sent these off to the time capsule," he went on, walking the aisles, putting the time lines on kids' desks. "They seemed so right for it. But I decided you'd want to show them off, in time, to your own children."

"I'm going to show mine off to the bottom of the wastebasket," Nick whispered.

A bee flew in the window and started diving at kids, who screamed and dodged.

"OK, calm down," Mr. Star called. "That bee's not interested in you. There's not a one of you sweet enough." The bee must have heard him, because it swooped at his bald spot like it was a landing strip. He ducked but kept on talking. "And here are the papers you all wrote on the first day of school. Marshall, I think you're today's monitor. Please hand these out."

Marshall's nose was just below desk level, where he was digging out paper airplanes. Most of them looked like they'd been prechewed.

"Marshall, I'm talking to you!"

Dumping a handful of crashed planes in the basket, Marshall took the stack of papers from Mr. Star and read the top one to himself. Then he began to laugh. "You guys aren't going to believe this," he told us. "They're even weirder than time lines."

Mr. Star headed to the back of the room to look for more junk for us to drag home as Marshall handed back the funny stuff.

"Couldn't you die!" Lisa said, crumpling up her First-Day-of-School. "I sound so *immature*! What'd you write?" she called to Molly, who shrugged and reached around my shoulder for Lisa's paper. Lisa smoothed out the crumpled ball and handed it over.

The friendly 4B bee started doing killer gymnastics between us, and Molly pulled back. So I

29

just took Lisa's paper and read out loud. "What I am going to get out of 4th grade," it said at the top. I remembered that one. That was when we were new in Mr. Star's class and scared. Holding it out to the side, I read on as Molly and Lisa grabbed for it. "I don't want truble with this one grup of girls," it said. "Last year I had a lot of truble. I—"

Molly jerked it away, leaving me a thumbful of paper. "Spy," she hissed.

Like a good spy, I read Molly's "What I am going to get" over her shoulder because she wasn't covering it with her hand. "I plan to get all A's again. At the end of the year I plan to have all the math done and get extra credit." She'd done it, too.

Nick made a ball out of his and lobbed it into the wastebasket while Mr. Star's back was turned. The bee buzzed in, probably thinking he'd discovered a huge new flying flower.

I couldn't remember what I'd written. It seemed like a million years ago that we'd been that young. Before handing me my paper, Marshall read it and shook his head. "Yeah, well, take away the kickball, and I guess you're right."

In incredibly bad handwriting it said, "At the end of 4th, I want to be the same. Except better at kickball." I stuck my foot out to trip Marshall, but he'd already moved on.

Probably it was true, though. I guess I knew a little more about China, maybe. And multiplication. But I sure wasn't much taller. Or bigger. Nick was still my best friend. And Molly was still the girl I liked about as much as a pop quiz. What's more, I figured that at the end of the summer I'd *still* be the same. Except I might make time-capsule history as the most boring kid in 4B.

# 4

# Is It Alive?

A paper star nipped me in the neck, curved around, and landed on the floor at my feet. It was covered with red R.P.s.

"Sorry," Rolf Pfutzenreuter called from across the room. "I meant to get Molly." Maybe, but I doubt it. Rolf's got good star control.

We'd made it to the last day of 4B. And even though there were *two* teachers in our room, I'd still gotten zapped by a folded paper star. The place was a hive of 4Bs.

Nobody was sitting down. Michelle was pulling thumbtacks out of the Animals of the Sahara Desert chart. Althea was packing the cactus plants in a cardboard box. A whole cluster of kids was helping Miss Ivanovitch collapse the chair she'd brought with her once when she'd subbed for Mr. Star. It was one of those canvas chairs that are supposed to fold easy as zip, but something had got stuck. On the back of it was written, "The Great Oz." It was weird. All of us liked it. Mr. Star liked it too. He liked it so much, she'd left the chair for him to use, and he'd stretched it all out of shape. She wasn't taking it home, though, just moving it down the hall, because next year she was teaching fifth. Full-time. Not just subbing, but teaching every day.

"Hey, you guys, guess what I found in the back of my desk!" Nick held up a long wooden paint stirrer. The whole class looked at it and groaned, even Mr. Star. Especially Mr. Star. That wasn't just any old paint stirrer from the hardware store. It was the class bathroom pass, and it had been missing for two months. Mr. Star had painted on it in big yellow letters, "Bathroom Pass, 4B," and you had to have it when you left so Mr. Star could be sure that only one kid was gone at a time. When it got lost, Mr. Star told us no one could leave class to go until the pass was found. After a couple of days, though, and a few emergencies, he just made another pass and colored the letters green this time so nobody could cheat.

Mr. Star took the stirrer and shook his head as he turned it over. I thought for a minute he was going to whack Nick's bottom with it. But he just handed it back. "Keep it, Nick. To remember Four B," he said.

Another four-pointed paper star caught the cardboard glass of milk on the Food Groups mobile. It spun around. Fast food.

"OK, friends," Mr. Star called, "Enough's enough.

You have exactly three seconds to get back to your seats. One . . . two . . ."

We scrambled to our desks, and the hive stopped buzzing. The last day of school, and we still hadn't found out what would happen to us if he counted all the way to three. Something awful. Like maybe he had this button on his desk that he'd push if we didn't sit down in time, and a trap door in the floor would open and we'd drop down past the cafeteria under us into this place in the middle of the earth where wormy monsters would turn us into toe jam. Either that or he'd make us miss recess. One or the other.

Actually, he *could* have counted three while we were still diving for our desks, but instead he just went on. "Stash those galaxies in your grocery sacks or in the green trash bag at the door. Do it now! I want no more star wars. Ever."

Just about everybody had made at least three paper stars in the past month. Marshall, who's big on origami, had shown us how to fold them out of two pieces of notebook paper. You count down five lines, fold on the fifth line, and like that. Nobody had to teach us how to throw them, though. You toss them points up and not flat out like a Frisbee. Some kids had painted stripes, dots, or initials on theirs with markers. Mine had zigzags. Molly didn't

34

make even one, but she had one of my zigzaggers in the pocket of her notebook. I'd watched her hide it there. Maybe she stuck pins in it or something to jinx me in kickball. I don't know why else she'd want it.

Cleaning out my desk, I had found, so far, fifteen stars, as well as two pink erasers pocked with pencil-dug caves, a letter I was supposed to take home October ninth inviting my folks to Open House, and a piece of Jolly Rancher Fruit Punch Stix stuck to wads of used Kleenex. Maybe small creatures with runny noses were living in the dark corners of my desk.

"People," Mr. Star called, waving the attendance sheet, "Eugene is the only one absent. What do you know about Eugene?"

Nick raised his hand. "What I know about Eugene is that he's this kid with black bangs, about four foot four, who's . . ."

Mr. Star grinned, then sighed and said, "Nick, this is not comedy time. It's wind-down time."

Nick shrugged. "Probably he's sick. Hobie and I'll clear out his desk and locker for him."

"Good," Mr. Star said, checking the sheet. "You do that. And since you're all so busy, I'll take the attendance down to the office myself today. Miss Ivanovitch will be here with you. And get those science books lined up neatly on the shelf." Glancing at the mirror by the door, he pushed a few hairs over the bald spot on the top of his head.

As he left the room, Miss Ivanovitch brushed her very thick black hair out of her face and beamed at us. "When *I* want your attention today," she said brightly, "I'll do this." From her skirt pocket she pulled out a three-inch yellow-plastic biplane and put it to her lips. Looking out over all of us, she took a deep breath, held it about half a minute, and then blew into the plane's tail. Propellers whirling, the airplane started to whine like a fire siren, *whOOOoo-ee, whoo-eEEEeeeee*.

She got it. Our attention. No problem.

"I have an announcement," she told us while the whine wound down. "I didn't know how I was going to scoot Mr. Star out of the room, but he went all by himself." She smiled like she thought that was pretty amazing. "I told him I was coming to get things ready for next year, and that's true, but mostly I'm here for his surprise party. I've brought Hawaiian Punch and a box of graham crackers—"

"Graham crackers! Eeeuuu!" Molly stopped talking to Lisa long enough to moan. "Those are for when you're sick."

"They're very healthy," Miss Ivanovitch told her, ripping open the box. "Look, I'll get them out on

36

a plate and pour the punch as fast as I can. You keep cleaning. I hope you don't mind the paper cups. They have bunnies on them, but they were all I had at home."

"Why does she have to surprise Mr. Star?" Molly whispered to Lisa. "I don't like it. I don't like *her*. She's trying to get him to like her. I *know* it."

Then she turned to Miss Ivanovitch. "OK, why are you having a party for Mr. Star? It's the last day of school. Why not a party for us?"

Miss Ivanovitch shook her head. Her earrings, which looked like carrots, wobbled. "Oh, it's for all of you, too, of course," she said, "but I thought you knew. Today is Mr. Star's birthday!"

"You're kidding!" Molly tossed her head back and crossed her arms. "What I want to know is how she learns things like that," she told Lisa. Molly was always telling people that she knew Mr. Star's telephone number, like she called him practically every night to get the homework answers. Big deal. It was probably in the phone book.

"We can't have a party. I don't have a present." Molly peered into her empty desk, maybe expecting a box tied with a blue bow to suddenly be there.

"The last day of school is a kind of present," Miss Ivanovitch said with a sigh, as a yellow-striped star whizzed past her nose.

"And so, onward!" she declared, carefully placing a wet sponge and a shaker of Comet on Marshall's desk. He sprinkled some out and began to scrub. She walked back to the sink and started pouring pink punch into bunny cups.

"Comet," Marshall sang as he pushed the sponge across his desk, "it makes your teeth turn green. Comet, it tastes like gasoline. Comet, it makes you vomit. So try some Comet and vomit to-daaaaay."

Kids sat talking about whether or not to toss out little pieces of wax, ratty baseball cards, and the clay pencil holders they'd made in art. Molly and Lisa gathered up the science books, and Nick and I headed into the hall to clean the junk out of Eugene's locker.

Eugene had locker number 37, next to Rolf's. We'd already turned in our locks, so no problem getting it open, at least. It was mess city. Out of the bottom we dragged a stiff winter boot, a strap without a backpack, a mountain of old math sheets, lots of Band-Aid wrappers with the little red strings hanging off, and a Hills Brothers coffee can filled with those markers that smell like the color they are. Its lid was poked full of holes, like the markers inside were hamsters and had to breathe. Everything but the coffee can we tossed into the garbage.

Then, on the top shelf of the locker, under a wadded-up red Central School sweatshirt, we found this shoe box. Eugene had written on it in grape marker, "Keep in a dark place." It was dark in the top of his locker, all right, and there was a funny smell.

We put the box on the floor and stuffed the coffee can inside the sweatshirt, figuring we could pile the junk from Eugene's desk in the shirt, too. We didn't have any more sacks. Then we sat down and carefully opened the shoe box.

It's a good thing we were sitting. If we hadn't been, what we found in the box would have knocked us over.

"Is it alive?" Nick asked.

"Alive and growing bigger every day," I told him. "I think it's moving."

"Will it kill you?"

"I'm not sure," I said. "Probably not unless you eat it, and I, for one, am not going to."

We both knew what it was, though. It was a birthday present for Mr. Star.

"It stinks a little," Nick said.

"It smells like what it is, that's all," I told him, holding the box out at arm's length and wishing my arm was longer.

We left Eugene's locker open to prove it was empty and ready for someone in next year's fourth grade. Then we carried the stuffed sweatshirt and the covered box back into the room.

Everything seemed pretty normal. Nobody was

throwing stuff out the windows or anything. So
that we'd be finished before Mr. Star got back, Nick
scrubbed both his desk and mine, humming the
Comet song to pass the time. I settled down under
the back table with Eugene's purple marker and
graped in the whole top of the shoe box. When I
was finished, you couldn't read "Keep in a dark
place" at all. Didn't look bad, and the marker smell
almost killed the queer stink of the stuff inside.

"What are you doing down there?" Molly asked,
sticking her head under the table.

"It's a surprise," I told her, knowing that now,
at least, it wouldn't be a secret.

"Come out!" she ordered. "We're planning a
little surprise ourselves now for Miss I've Got an
Itch."

"Ivanovitch," I told her. "Cut it out, Molly.
She's OK."

"Sure, if you say so. Anyway, we're going to flat-
drop books at ten o'clock, so you better get out."

As I moved back to my chair, I saw that everybody, no matter where they were sitting or standing, was holding a science book. And almost
everybody was grinning. Miss Ivanovitch, her back
to us, was piling stacks of graham crackers on a
small tray.

The room got quieter and quieter, but Miss Ivanovitch just kept stacking graham crackers. The kids stared at the clock. Five seconds to ten, four seconds, three, two . . . one . . .

*SPLAT!* The books fell into the quiet, and Miss Ivanovitch jumped about a mile. Graham crackers scattered at her feet. She turned around and her eyes were wide.

Mr. Star's were narrow. He stood at the door and zapped each of us with a stare.

Kids looked everywhere but at him—at the ceiling, in the wastebasket, out the window at the ball on the cafeteria roof. Molly and Lisa started polishing their desk tops. Marshall dived into the shattered graham crackers and blew floor fuzz off each piece he picked up.

The room was quiet a whole minute before Miss Ivanovitch spoke. Looking especially *interested*, she said, as if she'd just won a bet, "It still works!"

"Works?" Mr. Star glared out at twenty-five innocent kids and down at the twenty-five science books flat on the floor. The science books were clearly not stacked neatly on the shelf. His forehead was all lines. "What still works?"

"The law of gravity," she told him. "You know, like apples falling down from trees, not up."

"I know the law of gravity," he said, a strange look on his face.

"Well, I expect this was a gravity check the children devised, because if the law hadn't worked, those science books would have been flying all over the place." She picked up the closest one, turned it over, and dropped it flat. "Well, now that we've not broken any laws, it's time to move on." Mr. Star shook his head as she stepped up on a footstool next to the door and took a little breath. Molly let out a big breath and sat down.

*Who-eeEEEEEEE-WHO-eeeeeee.* Miss Ivanovitch blew on the small plane. Its propellers spun. I wondered if gravity made it work. "Group," she asked us, "don't you have something to say to Mr. Star?"

Everybody was quiet, and I wondered, for a minute, if we were supposed to say, "I'm sorry."

"Happy birthday," she mouthed.

"Happy birthday, Mr. Star," we said in the same singsong we used every school morning of the year to say, "Good morning, Mr. Star."

"Why, thank you, class. I'd thought that was a secret." He ran his fingers over the top of his head and smiled a little. "By the way, those crumbs," he said, pointing at the ones Marshall had left on the floor. "Were they part of the gravity check, too?"

Miss Ivanovitch shook her head. "Actually, they were more of an accident. They're birthday cake.

If we break the clean ones in two, there'll still be enough for everyone to have a bite. I expect we don't need to dip into the pieces Marshall rescued from the floor."

Kids grabbed and drank and swallowed cracker bits whole.

"Uh," Nick said, fairly loud, "Mr. Star, there's something on your desk." I'd put the box there and then moved around to the other side of the room. Nick didn't exactly say it was a birthday present, and he didn't exactly say it was from him and me, either.

"You *got* him something?" Molly asked, looking at the freshly markered box. "No fair."

"I bet it's full of, like, ratty old paper stars," Lisa said. "I bet."

"You bet wrong," I told her.

Mr. Star smiled, all warm and kindly, as though he'd decided we were nice children after all. As though he thought maybe this box had a million dollars in it, or at least some homemade chocolate-chip cookies, or a new tie that glowed in the dark. He looked so pleased that I began to feel sick.

He wasn't going to be pleased much longer.

In the box was a science experiment. A couple of months before, Mr. Star had given each of us a piece of whole wheat butter-crust bread. Some of us were supposed to put our bread in the refrigerator for a week. Some of us put it in the sun. Some of us had to rub the bread on the floor, sprinkle it with water, and hide it in a dark place. That's the group Eugene had been in, the dirt-and-dark group. But he must have been absent when everybody brought their bread to class and discovered that dirt and dark make things grow on bread that sun and cold don't—spidery, gaggish threads of mold. All the D & D slices we'd looked at were disgusting after one week. Eugene's bread had been hiding out for two *months*.

"Do you think," Nick whispered to me, "they'd send me home from Mighty Byte Camp if I let some of that stuff grow between my toes?"

"This is very thoughtful of you, class," Mr. Star said, eyeing the purple-topped box. "It won't make me fat, will it?"

"Oh, no, Mr. Star, it won't do that," Nick told him.

"It's from *all* of us," Molly said loud before Mr. Star had a chance to lift the lid. She wasn't going to let Nick and me get away with giving Mr. Star a purple present when she didn't have anything to give him.

Nick sighed, like he was mad about it but what else could he do. "Sure, OK," he said.

"The whole room," I agreed.

44

Molly and Lisa beamed. Everybody gathered around close to watch Mr. Star open the class gift.

Kids leaned in to look, and as he lifted off the top there was this huge group gasp. They'd expected, maybe, double-fudge-mint brownies.

That must have been what Mr. Star had expected, too. His smile turned crooked, his eyes opened wide, and he sucked in his breath like he was about to say something. But while his mouth hung open, no words came out. He just stared down into the purple box.

"Gr-oss!" Marshall said. And I guess maybe that was the word for it. The creepy gray hairs of ancient mold had just about dissolved the bread they grew on and filled up all the corners of the box. You couldn't imagine that the gooey mess at the bottom had once been something you could spread peanut butter and jelly on.

Mr. Star looked up at the class, which was backing away as if what he was holding was a box of measles germs.

"This is . . . astonishing," he said, shaking his head.

"It's, like, a joke," Lisa told him, weakly, and a few people laughed.

"A *bad* joke," Molly said, looking at me like she thought I'd grown up in the box, too.

There was this long silence, so I figured I'd better try to get out of it. "Actually, it's a cure Eugene discovered for bald heads," I explained to Mr. Star. "And it's all yours. You may make millions."

Mr. Star ran his hand over his thinning hair and smiled. "I'm afraid the color's a little off," he said.

"Yeah, well, there's that," Nick agreed. "And to make it work, you have to sit on the top shelf of Eugene's locker for sixty days."

"We like you just the way you are, Mr. Star." Molly tried to take the shoe box away, but he held on.

"I think you should put it in the time capsule to eat up our interviews," I told him. "It seems to be hungry."

Then, with Miss Ivanovitch leading, we all sang, "Happy Birthday to You."

"Thanks," Mr. Star said, swigging down a bunny cup of punch. He stared into the fuzzy shoe box. "I want you to know that in all my years of teaching . . ." He shook his head and then, suddenly, smiled big. ". . . I've never seen a more splendid specimen of bread mold. It's outstanding. Just look at that. It's museum quality." He *liked* that box. He really liked it. "You don't happen to know, do you," he asked, "if Eugene added sugar?"

Then, grinning at Miss Ivanovitch, he raised his

empty cup high and started to do a kind of silly dance. "Happy birthday to meee," he sang. Almost all the kids groaned and looked away. It's embarrassing to watch your teacher show off. "Four B is hi-is-sto-ry," he sang on.

This time everybody cheered, and Miss Ivanovitch blew her whistle. "*And* her story," she added. "It's the last day of school for the girls, too. Listen, I can hardly wait to read your 'What I Did Last Summer' paragraphs next fall."

Mine was going to be short. "What I Did Last Summer. Nothing. The End."

"Four B is you-ur sto-ry," Mr. Star sang, even louder. "You'll *all* have great summers, If you don't skin your knee." At that all the kids clapped and yelled, "All *right*!" All but Nick and me.

# 5

## My Favorite Number Is Two-oo

"And here she is, folks, Stockton's very own sweetheart, all set to sing you her very own brand-new tune, the marvelous Molly Bosco! Molly is four feet seven and just loves school, and her dog's name is Spot. Give her, please, a warm, warm welcome!"

Guy Garron, official Miss Pre-Teen Personality M.C., clapped his hands like Molly was at the top of the charts. He had on a white suit, a red bow tie, and shiny black hair that you could tell was a wig. His smile looked like he'd bought it somewhere too, in size extra large. The Miss Pre-Teen Personality people had rented the Central School auditorium for their contest. Across the top of the stage they'd hung a banner that read "Stars of the Future."

As Guy Garron walked off, Molly rushed on, wearing this shiny sky-blue dress and a headband with wobbly antennas that had sparkling silver stars on the ends. She did look like something from the future. Seven other girls had gone before her. One of them had said a poem about this kid who wouldn't take the garbage out, a couple had sort of played the violin, one had tap danced to "Somewhere over the Rainbow," and the others had sung songs I couldn't hear much of with my ears covered. Now it was Molly's turn to be talented.

This was Nick's last day to be home before heading off to Mighty Byte. It was also his turn to be a grump.

"Why are we here?" he asked me. "Just tell me why. Give me one good reason."

Reasons number one and two crackled and rumbled outside, making the stage lights flicker and the floor shake. Water hit the roof like it was pouring from a giant pitcher. I mean, being there was something to *do* on a rainy day. Molly ducked, like she was scared a lightning bolt was going to part her hair down the middle.

Reason number three was that Molly's grandmother had bought twenty tickets at two dollars apiece and given us each one. Our moms had told us that Saturday afternoon or not, we should go because it was the *nice* thing to do. I'd thought it might be a laugh, but so far it was a bore, even though we had second-row seats.

"OK, Molly, let's get on with it," Guy Garron called from offstage. "Can't let a little water dampen our spirits, now can we!"

Molly eyed the ceiling, then turned around and nodded to the woman at the piano behind her. *TA-DA!* the woman played. Molly bowed, and Toby, who was sitting between Nick and me, began to clap.

"Not yet," I whispered to him. "Wait'll it's over or they'll know she paid you." Molly hadn't actually paid him to clap, but when she'd brought the tickets over, she'd given him a pouch of Big League Chew gum, the kind that's all shredded and tastes like watermelon, and then she'd showed him how to clap really loud by cupping his hands together instead of hitting flat. So he'd been practicing cupping hands and blowing eye-high bubbles.

The woman at the little upright piano began to play something that sounded a lot like "Happy Birthday to You." Molly took one step forward and went from glum to bright like somebody had turned on her switch.

"This is my song. I made it up so you could know all about me," she said, in a voice that showed she'd learned the speech by heart. "It is an original song. It is called 'My Personal Favorites.' "

Her personal favorites? Catchy. I couldn't believe it. What was she going to sing about? Her favorite socks? Her favorite yogurt flavor? She must have taken me seriously when I asked if she was going to write a song about her favorite colors and numbers. I couldn't hold my ears against Molly, though. This I had to hear.

The piano player hit a chord and started again from the top. There may have been a change here and there, but the Molly Original Song was your basic "Happy Birthday" all the way. Toby hummed along as Molly sang, "My favorite color is blue, Ooooo-ooo-oo-oo-oo-oo." To prove that was no lie, she grabbed at her blue dress. "I sure hope yours is, too," she went on, trying to smile as she sang, "Ooooo-ooo-oo-oo-oo-oo," which isn't easy. The stars on her headband wiggled and shone. Tony clapped again, the thunder grumbled, and Molly looked scared, not like Molly at all. Her voice shook, but she sang on.

"My favorite number is two." She held up two fingers. "My favorite food is beef stew." As she stirred this imaginary pot, I wondered if it was really true about the beef stew.

"My favorite instrument is a kazoo." She took one out of her pocket and hummed, faintly, Oooo-ooo-ooo-oooo-oooo-oo. Somehow, she and the piano player never came to the end of the line at the same time. Then she sucked in a big breath for the final push. "Though I've lots of personal favorites, my favorite letter is U." She pointed to the audience. At first I thought it was me she was pointing at,

52

but she probably couldn't even see us from the stage.

Grabbing the edges of her skirt, she crossed one foot behind the other and kind of bobbed up and down, shaking her starry feelers from side to side like she was part of a cuckoo clock. "Brava!" Molly's grandmother called. "Brava, Molly!" She and Toby clapped the loudest. There couldn't have been more than forty of us in the audience, all clustered down near the front. I guess the Miss Pre-Teen Personality Contest wasn't first on many people's lists of Saturday-afternoon things to do, even if somebody *had* given them tickets. Maybe that's why Molly didn't exactly get a round of applause. More like a triangle.

"She was good," Toby said. "I know her," he told the woman in front of us, who was rooting for the tap dancer. I gave his head a knuckle rub, which slowed him down some. But then he started to sing to Molly's original melody, "Roogie-roogie-roo-roo, Boogie-boogie-boo-boo!"

"Catchy tune," Nick said. "My favorite sick is the flu," he sang.

"My favorite stick is with glue," I tried. We could have gone on and on with kangaroo, tattoo, boo-boo, and ka-choo, but by then Guy Garron was back, scooping Molly off the stage.

"And now," he yelled, like we were a mass of

thousands, "for your delight—and for the approval of those ever-important judges—here is our ninth and final contestant in the talent portion of the Local Miss Pre-Teen Personality Contest. May I present to you that four-foot-one-inch, ten-year-old dynamo whose parakeet's name is Waldo, that star of the future, Lisa Soloman!"

Not the Lisa Soloman we know, I thought. She wouldn't dare be in a contest against Molly. I knew she wouldn't dare. Molly had practically told me so.

The woman at the piano played something snappy, and out this kid tumbled, cartwheeling across the stage in a black-and-yellow tiger leotard that kind of sparkled in the light. It was our Lisa, all right.

"If Lisa wins, that's trouble," Nick whispered to me. "Molly won't let any of the girls talk to her again, ever. She might as well move to the Sahara Desert." Since first grade Molly had been Boss of the Girls. Losing had *never* been her favorite thing. The contest was getting interesting.

Lisa stood on her hands and then, somehow, pretzeled herself into a circle and rolled across the stage.

Toby stood up on his seat and clapped with cupped hands. Molly hadn't counted on that. A lot of other people clapped, too. Lisa was pretty amazing. The storm thundered outside, but Lisa bounced up, beaming like sunshine. Then, whirling around on her toes, she came down in a split. I wondered if the old stage had splinters in it. If it did, she was going to wind up with at least two wooden legs.

She kept moving as the music got faster, twisting around like a bendable rubber Gumby that can put his elbows in his ears and his nose on his toes. She did stuff that would snap me in half and smiled the whole time.

Her folks were at the end of our row looking proud, and when she bowed, her dad threw her a cellophane-wrapped bunch of pink daisies. Molly's grandmother, two seats away from us, tightened her mouth and folded her hands in her lap.

"Lisa's the best," Toby said, clapping his loudest clap. "I know her, too. She's Molly's best friend," he told the woman in front of us.

"At least she used to be," Nick said.

If this had been a contest on TV, like for Miss Universe, it would have been time for the shampoo commercial. The first heat was over. But since Miss Pre-Teen P. wasn't on the air, Guy Garron came out to entertain us with the rules.

"Each and every one of these young ladies is the cream of Stockton," he told us, rubbing his hands together. "Frankly, I'd hoped we'd have more contestants from a town this size, but these girls certainly were terrific, weren't they?" He waited for clapping, and there was a little. "They know they

55

are the Stars of the Future!" With one hand he pointed to the banner above him, and with the other he pointed offstage to where the future stars waited. "The winner of this contest will have her own gorgeous float in the Fourth of July parade. She'll get a wonderful, wonderful gift certificate from Lyman's drugstore, a free lunch at the Chuckwagon, a pair of fancy anklets from Here's Josie, and much more. On top of that, she'll go on to the state pageant in Carbondale July seventh, where she'll do her little act and have an interview onstage with a famous radio personality. So, to prepare her for that big interview, and to help today's judges decide on the Stockton Miss Pre-Teen Personality, I'm going to ask our little girls each the same question. Just watch their pre-teen personalities shine." He grinned like a good Guy, tugged at his red bow tie, and called, "Come on back, girls!"

All nine of them filed on. The piano played "When You Wish upon a Star." Lisa was still carrying the daisies. She was at one end of the line. Molly was at the other. They were smiling, but not at each other.

"You can all think about the question for a minute, and then each of you will give a little answer. Ready?" The piano *TA-DA*ed. "Listen closely, now. I want each of you lovely little ladies to tell me your hopes for the *future*." He pointed again to the

56

banner. "What does the future mean to *you*?" The piano started in on the theme from *Star Wars*.

A *little* answer he wanted? I couldn't have done it. I would have uh-ed and ah-ed all over the place. The *future*? This was going to be embarrassing. I slid down in my chair and closed my eyes. It didn't help.

The girl who'd said the poem looked at the stage floor and mumbled. "Louder, Tiffany," her mother called out, and Tiffany stopped talking altogether. Toby began to squirm in his seat.

Molly was up next. "If I could wish upon a star," she started, using the words of the song they'd walked in with, "I would make sure we *have* a future by doing away with wars and making everybody in the world friends with every other body . . . in the world."

I looked up. That was all. It wasn't as bad as it could have been. It wasn't as bad as I would have done. A few people said, "Awwww," like they thought she was sweet.

"Can we go now?" Toby asked.

The other girls wanted kindness, friends, and good grades so they could get into the college of their choice.

"I've got to go to the bathroom," Toby whispered loud.

"Wait," I told him. I wanted to hear Lisa.

Nick knew Toby well enough to know that waiting would mean a natural disaster. He got up and scooted Toby across the row of people's feet. I followed, mumbling excuse me's.

"Down in front," somebody hissed.

We missed the first part, but at the top of the aisle I stopped and listened to the end of Lisa's speech.

". . . and in the future, I plan to win the State Miss Pre-Teen Personality Contest, and go on to be on the TV show for the national contest, and get discovered for, like, Hollywood or one of the really good soaps."

What a stupid thing to say! I moaned and ducked out the door. Nick and Toby were in the hall. Toby's green shorts were soggy.

Nick rolled his eyes at me. "We were too late by two seconds. How'd things go in there?"

"Lisa just blew it," I told him. "You know how Molly talked about world peace and stuff? Well, Lisa said she wanted to be on TV."

Outside, the sky was white, not gray anymore. It was only about three o'clock, and we still had time to sail a few leaf boats and old paper stars down the gutter streams. The rain that was still falling sure wasn't going to get Toby any wetter.

As we started out, I heard clapping. I wanted to

find out what had happened, even though I was pretty sure Molly had won with her speech. "Wait up, will you?" I said to Nick. "I want to see how Lisa takes it."

Sure enough, Molly was standing there at the front of the stage with Guy Garron, her teeth set in a smile.

"Isn't she *wonderful!*" he said. "Such a *sweet* little song! And such a *nice* little speech!" People clapped lightly, like the sound of rain sprinkling. The piano played "When You Wish upon a Star" again. That was about all I could take, and I was just pushing the door open again when he went on. "If, for any reason, our Miss Pre-Teen Personality for today is not able to go to Carbondale for the state contest, little Molly here, as runner-up, will take her place." He patted Molly on her antennaed head.

I thought for a minute that little Molly might snap at him. If she was runner-up, that meant she hadn't won. I couldn't believe it.

"And now . . ." The piano player ran her thumb down all the keys. ". . . The big winner, the brightest little star of this town, who charmed us all with her wish to win . . . Miss Local Pre-Teen Personality . . . Lisa Soloman!"

Lisa jumped up and down, squealing and clapping her hands in front of her face. Then she cart-

wheeled to the front of the stage next to Molly. The piano played "Thank Heaven for Little Girls."

"Come *onnnnn!*" Toby called, as he and Nick opened the auditorium door all the way. Somebody turned around and shushed us.

Lisa was still bouncing like she was on a trampoline. On TV, Molly would have been hugging her and looking like she'd wanted Lisa to win more than anything. But this wasn't TV. Molly had moved away as though Lisa smelled the way Toby did.

"I want to thank my gymnastics coach, Mr. Boyle; my mother and father, who gave me these flowers; my . . ." Lisa cooed on. We banged the door shut for the last time and headed into the fresh air.

"So," Nick said, as we sloshed down the street, "you know what that means. That means Molly will be free all summer. Like you. Maybe you can do things together. Ha ha," he said.

"Ha ha," I said back. "Me and Molly. Ha ha." No way.

"Ha ha," Toby said, and blew a bubble of gum so gigantic that when it broke, it collapsed into his eyelashes. He must have had the whole shredded pack in his mouth. Of course then he rubbed his eyes with his fists and made it worse. His tears didn't dissolve the stuff, either, so Nick and I had to make a fireman's seat with our hands linked and carry him the rest of the way home.

"I sure don't want to go away," Nick said, as we let Toby loose at his front steps. "But if you think about it, even Mighty Byte has got to be better than this."

June 23

Dear Hobie,

This place stinks. My teacher's name is Mr. Button. He lives in a house. I live in a tent. I wrote my dad and told him I wanted to come home. He wrote me back and said forget it.

They talk funny here. You're not going to believe this. They call breakfast A.M. Input. Most of the kids are really into computers. All they talk about is bits and bytes and bugs. Free time they call "Forced Fun," because they'd rather be sitting at the green screens.

There are lots of bugs here besides the kind that mess up computers. The mosquitos are the size of Marshall's airplanes. Even their bytes are big. Get it? Ha. Ha. The bugs on the lagoon are better at walking on it than I am at canoeing on it. And there are mega grasshoppers. I've been trying to get a grasshopper race started, but so far I haven't found many people interested in making bugs jump out of circles.

The food is gross. Computers probably made it. How's Tom Sawyer? I bet your toes are dirty. WRITE ME LETTERS!!!!!

Nick

P.S.   I haven't met Cindy. Ha.

P.P.S.   This one nutty guy in my tent is called Roger. He folds his dirty clothes.

P.P.P.S.   Tell Toby to study hard so he can come here next year and I can stay home so we can win the pie-eating contest on the 4th of July. Don't shoot off too many rockets.

# 6

# Afloat

The summer hadn't taken off like rockets, but already it was my birthday. The Fourth of July—all-day celebration. I was standing in front of City Hall in the middle of the action. A block or so away the parade was forming up, and two bands were practicing different songs. Down Central Street, blocked off from traffic for the parade, bikes weaved back and forth, their spokes threaded through with red, white, and blue crepe paper. Grandparents in folding chairs sat along the curb waiting for little kids to march by waving little flags. Two firecrackers popped, and a couple of guys ran like crazy to prove they'd had nothing to do with it.

Later, in the park, there'd be races, games, pony rides, bingo, a talent show, lots of food. And then, in the dark, fireworks. A birthday party. For the country. Not for me.

It seemed like summer had been around for years. I'd read about fifteen library books and taught Toby that one skunk plus two skunks make three skunks and one big stink. But this would probably be my best summer day. Maybe backpacking with my folks later would be OK, but other than that . . . It's hard to have fun by yourself.

Still, I'd told my folks I didn't want a birthday party. I mean, paper plates and plastic whistles and balloons are for babies. Besides, nobody was around for me to invite. So I'd gotten practical presents with my breakfast bran flakes and bananas—a blue shirt and an alarm clock. Anyway, the whole day is a party, right?

Wrong. The best day of the summer, and I was baby-sitting Toby. His folks and mine are in this really stupid lawn-mower drill team that marches in every Fourth of July parade, so Toby was mine until the parade was over.

"Hobie, look at me—I'm a rhino!" he yelled, waving a foamy white arm. He was standing with about eight other kids in water up to his knees. A stack of soapsuds wobbled on top of his head.

Somebody had poured detergent into the big fountain in front of City Hall, and the pool under it was a humungous pan of bubbles. Suds exploded from the six-foot fountain spray. Probably it was high-school kids who'd done it. A couple of times every summer somebody soaps the fountain when nobody's looking. The high-school kids usually stick around long enough to pour in the whole bottle, and this sure was a whole-bottle job.

"Hobie, look, now I'm a dandelion!" Toby called, piling more foam on his head. "Blow on me and make a wish." *He* blew, but his suds hat stayed put.

Puffy gobs of soap hung for a while in the air, stuck in trees, and floated onto the grass. Kids, not all of them little, jumped into the fountain with their clothes on and climbed out looking like Creatures from Slime Lagoon. Then they patted on bubble muscles and beards and ran into the crowd to show off.

"Come on, Tobe, time to get out and see the clowns," I called. "They're really funny."

Actually, clowns are never funny. When I was his age I used to run away from them. The one working his way toward us had on a rainbow wig, a polka-dot suit, and a rat face. He was taking Polaroid pictures of people and giving them away with a card from Phelps Photo.

Turning my back to the clown so he wouldn't shoot me, I leaned as far over the fountain pool as I dared and grabbed Toby, very carefully, by the wrist. I didn't want to go through the wash cycle. Toby's hand oozed through mine. Slick and easy.

I stood up straight. "Out!" I snarled, mean and vicious.

"I wish Nick was here. He's more fun than you." Toby sat down. Soap came up to his chin.

Down the block the kazoo band played "Be Kind to Your Webfooted Friends, For That Duck May Be Somebody's Mother."

"The parade is starting," I told him. "You'll miss the clowns in fat shoes and the floats and your mother pushing a lawn mower around in figure eights."

I stood up on the pool ledge. The only parade in sight was a big dog in a straw hat running away from a girl in a Raggedy Ann wig.

Soon, though, I saw two marchers. Before the bands, before the mayor, before the parade, Marshall and Trevor were jogging down the street handing out leaflets. They were wearing big, round smiley-face sandwich boards their mothers must have made. "We do windows," it said on Marshall's sign where the smiley face's smile should have been. "We cut grass," it said on Trevor's. I wondered if they were making a bundle. They sure were busy. Every time I'd called one of them, they were busy.

Before long, the first band came. After that from the fountain ledge I watched the Little League teams march past, tossing balls across one another. Their uniforms said stuff like Murray's Hardware and Lee's Restaurant, and they looked like they were having a good time.

"Hey, Hobe!" R.X. called, and I waved.

Then came the Cub Scouts trying to keep in step,

kids in the park district day camps, and wavy lines of girls in pink fake-leather boots twirling batons up and missing them as they fell down.

Toby was the only kid still in the fountain. "If you drown or dissolve in there," I warned him, "your folks won't let me sit you again."

I wanted to get down where the action was so I could see Miss Pre-Teen Lisa, and our folks dressed up in kerchiefs and jeans pushing lawn mowers that had fake bulls' horns taped to their handles. Every year about twenty parent types dress up like something different and do half lefts and half rights and turnabouts and stuff pushing those ancient foot-powered lawn mowers. Last year they were Uncle Sams and Statues of Liberty. This year the theme was rodeo. They were dressed like cowpeople, my mom said. I mean, they were *parents,* doing stuff like that.

"I tell you what, I'll give you a nickel to get out," I called over my shoulder.

"Hey, Barfy!" "What you doing this summer?" two kids yelled. I nearly fell in the pool. I hadn't been Barfy since second grade. The Mar-Vor Marvels, smiley faces over their bellies, remembered that far back. Marshall handed me one of their leaflets.

"Right now I'm watching this kid," I said, nodding toward Toby, trying to ignore the "Barfy" stuff. I made an airplane out of the paper and sailed it out into the parade. "But I tell you what I'm going to do. I'm going to give you one whole dime to get in the nice cool water and pull the kid out."

"What kid?" Trevor asked. And when I whirled around and looked, Toby's arms weren't waving and his head was not sticking out of a suds mountain. He was nowhere.

"Toby!" I cried over the band music. Nothing. And to think I'd *teased* him about drowning!

I was about to belly flop in and practice lifesaving when he peeked around the base of the fountain and yelled, "Fooled you!"

I narrowed my eyes at him, grim as Mr. Star on a bad day.

"Nick would have laughed," he said, sliding under deeper.

"Make that a quarter," I told Marshall.

He laughed so hard his smiley board shook. "Maybe for three fifty," he told me.

Toby kicked a tidal wave at us.

"And then again, maybe not." Marshall and Trevor backed away.

Tom Sawyer would have got them to do it easy, I thought. If my dad wanted me to so bad, I'd try the Tom Sawyer stuff. "Would you drag him out,"

I asked them, "if I gave you a dead rat on a string?"

"You're kidding," Trevor said. He looked at me like he thought I'd had a flat in my brain. "You *got* a dead rat on a string?"

"No. I just wondered."

"We gotta go," Marshall said, and they did. Fast.

Then I remembered that Tom Sawyer didn't give that kid a dead rat for painting his fence. He conned the kid into giving *him* the rat. I was doing it wrong. Tom Sawyer got stuff off kids and then watched them do his whitewash job. And this was a kind of whitewash job.

"Lee-sa, Lee-sa, Lee-sa," some girls were chanting across the street. Michelle, Jenny, and a couple of other used-to-be-fourth-grade girls were waving their arms and shouting. "Lee-sa, Lee-sa!" And sure enough, there she was. It wasn't exactly the float Guy Garron had said it would be. I'd expected, maybe, a truck bed covered with Kleenex-stuffed chicken wire like the float the Historical Society had. The Kleenex on theirs was green like pale grass, and Abraham Lincoln stood on it waving and leaning on a fake ax. Actually, Lisa was in a car. A convertible, but still a car. Pinwheels spun on the front fenders and a hand-lettered sign on the door said, *Lisa Soloman, Local Miss Pre-Teen Personality*. There were too many words crammed onto such a little poster, so it was hard to read unless you already knew what it said.

Even Lisa wasn't what I expected. She didn't look like Lisa. Her hair was all snake curls, and her pink dress was the kind this kindergarten girl had worn in my cousin's wedding. All ruffles. The little kid in the wedding had thrown rose petals on the floor for the bride to walk on. Lisa was throwing kisses and frozen smiles. It was hard to tell who she was aiming them at. I sure didn't catch any.

Leaning in the hardware-store doorway, behind Michelle, Jenny, and the rest of the "Lee-sa" screamers, I could see Molly standing by herself eating a Popsicle. She saw me staring at her and tried to step farther back, but there wasn't any farther back to step into. So she waved, instead, waited a second, and then headed toward me, brushing past the girls, crossing the street just behind Lisa's amazing floatmobile.

Something was funny. The girls didn't follow Molly. They didn't even call, "Hi!" to her. They just kept yelling, "Lee-sa!"

"Hello, Hobart," she said, taking a small bite from her purple Popsicle.

"If I did that, my teeth would kill," I told her.

"What're you doing?" she asked. "Catching flies like Tom Sawyer?"

"I'm trying to get Toby out of the stupid bathtub, if you want to know." I hopped onto the ledge of the pool.

"You were good at that contest, Molly," Toby called to her. "I clapped loud."

"Yes," Molly said, "I know. Anyway," she went on, kicking the suds on the sidewalk, "I wanted to thank you guys for getting up and walking out when Lisa was making her dumb speech. At least now I know who my real friends are."

Me? Molly's real friend? She had to be kidding. I almost told her the real reason we'd left. But I didn't.

Across the street the girls moved along slowly, following Lisa's float, waving and yelling. The flags on the lampposts waved, too.

"Get *out*!" I told Toby. "I mean it! I'm going to count to three. One—two—"

"Three!" Toby yelled. "That's not so great. I can count that far." It was those math lessons. The kid had a great teacher.

The air was full of booms from the big drum in the high-school band. The parade was passing me by. Then I remembered Tom Sawyer again.

"Hey, Molly," I said, treating her like a friend. A real friend. A true buddy I'd do a big favor for. "I bet you'd like to wade in and get Toby. Wouldn't that be fun?" She laughed like I was Saturday-morning cartoons, but I went on. "Just *maybe,* if you give me the rest of your Popsicle, I'll let you do it."

"You're kidding. You'll *let* me go in that stuff to get Toby if I give *you* my Popsicle?" I nodded, wondering if any kid outside a book was really as dumb as the guys Tom Sawyer knew.

"I'll think about it," she said.

From down the block we could hear the girls yelling clear and loud, "Lee-sa, Lee-sa!"

Molly must have thought about it as we listened. "Wow, Hobie, you're giving *me* that once-in-a-lifetime chance to wade into City Hall fountain? That's really nice of you." She smiled a kind of wacky smile. "Well, can you wait for the Popsicle until I get him out?"

She was going to do it. I couldn't believe she was going to do it. A smart girl like Molly had fallen for the old Tom Sawyer whitewash scam. And a Popsicle isn't even a dead rat.

Kicking her sandals off, she got up on the ledge next to me and held out the Popsicle. Toby edged closer.

Turning away from him, she asked, "So, what are you doing for the rest of the summer?"

I stomped on a batch of bubbles in the grass. "Oh, fool around. There's still the time capsule and all."

"That's just one day."

"Yeah, well. OK, what are you and Lisa and Jenny and Michelle planning?" I glanced down the block at the Lisamobile.

"Molly, I'm hungry," Toby said, and he stood up.

"Oh, I don't know for sure," she said, ignoring him. "My grandmother wants me to be a model, but I'm thinking about starting a business of some kind. I don't know what. I'll think of something."

Toby was almost in reach, so I grabbed at him. He bared his teeth and fell backward into the suds.

"When *is* Time Capsule Day, anyway?" Molly asked.

"Next Wednesday morning," I told her. "But you know, I think it's pretty dumb. Those future guys who dig that stuff up are going to think we're totally dull. Why aren't we burying something funny? You know, something—"

"Something weird?" she asked.

"Right. There's nothing weird in there that I know of, except maybe Lisa's smelly sticker."

"I'm a mushroom," Toby called out, heaping suds on top of his head.

"Are you poison?" Molly asked, waving the Popsicle in front of him.

"Yes." He scooted toward her. "You're not going to yank me out, are you?"

"Why would I do that?" she asked. The Popsicle dripped purple blood into the water.

"I want it," he said.

"Come and get it," she told him.

Behind us the fire engine cruised past slowly, part of the parade. Its siren moaned low, like it was headed toward a blinking firefly. Lisa was out of sight, somewhere beyond the hardware store.

"I've decided," Molly said, "that I'm going to the time capsule ceremony, too. I'm going to put something of my own in it. I can think of something better than a dumb smelly sticker. Like, I don't know . . . like maybe . . . my diary."

"Your *diary*? Oh, wow, I guess if anything's weird, that is," I said, trying to be nice.

She frowned. "Well, maybe not. My grandmother thinks I should get it published. I'll think of something." She licked the Popsicle.

"That's *mine*." Toby was mad.

"Who said?" She nibbled at it and stepped off the ledge.

Toby climbed out, following her. "Give it!"

She held the Popsicle high over his head while sudsy Toby tried to climb her like a tree.

"OK," she said, tossing the frozen gob to me. "I got him out. The Popsicle's all yours."

I caught it by the cold end and held it up out

75

of his reach. Purple ran down my arm and dripped off my elbow.

"You're mean!" Toby drowned out the fire engine with his wails.

The Popsicle smelled good, like grape Kool-Aid, and I wondered just for a second if Molly had conned me. But I probably wouldn't have eaten it anyway. I mean, she had been *licking* the sides. Besides, there wasn't even half of it left. So I gave the mushy mess to Toby, who used it to plug up his sound system.

"Hey, here comes your mother!" I told him. The grinding blades of lawn-mower bulls followed right on the tail of the fire engine. I grabbed Toby by his soggy T-shirt and dragged him over to the curb. And there they all were, yippee-ki-yi-yo-ing behind this guy carrying a sign, *Stockton's Very Famous Number-One Award-Winning Lawn-Mower Drill Team*. It was my dad who'd made the sign. It was embarrassing.

"Toby!" his mother yelled when she saw him waving. "What happened?"

"Oh, nothing," I called back, brushing a batch of violet foam off his ear. "Just a tiny bite from a very small mad dog."

"Not funny!" She ran her lawn mower into the curb and the very famous number-one award-winning drill team screeched to a halt.

As soon as they'd regrouped and churned on past, I rolled Toby's Big Wheel out from under the City Hall maple tree and he climbed on it. Molly followed me.

"Well, goodbye," I told her.

"Where are we going now?" she asked.

"I don't know where *you're* going. *I'm* taking Toby to his mom at the end of the parade. If she'll have him," I said. All the bubbles had blown off him or soaked in. He looked almost normal. Wet.

He stuck out a purple tongue and started pedaling down the sidewalk.

"Then what?" she asked.

"Then I'm going to the park. I want to be in line when Mr. Star sits in the dunk tank. I've saved my money to buy balls to throw."

"At Mr. Star? You wouldn't dare!"

"Wouldn't I?" I gave a mad Dracula laugh and rushed off after the Purple Speed Demon.

"I'll see you there," she called after.

Oh, no you won't, I thought. Not if I see you first.

# 7

# Bull's-Eye

At the entrance to the park bikes were chained to trees, to one another, or to nothing—just lying on their sides. Those were the rusted-out ones that kids knew nobody would *want* to steal. I'd walked. It wasn't all that far.

For about an hour I'd been on the phone trying to get guys to come with me. Rolf's cousin Thor was in town. R.X. had a team picnic. All the calls went like that. So it was going to be just one more free-kid summer afternoon. Well, almost free. I had five quarters in my pocket.

The day was hot and sweaty, but the air smelled pink. At the first booth this guy in a straw hat was yelling, "*Hey,* fifty cents, *hey,* fifty cents." He twirled a thin paper cone around the inside of this big spinning bowl until the cone was fat with cotton candy. The bees tumbling near it must have thought they'd died and gone to bee heaven. Cotton candy is really good. I like the way it gets hard and then disappears on your tongue, but I didn't buy any. I was saving my money.

Everything looked Fourth of July. The food and game booths were all draped with red-white-and-blue-striped paper. A fleet of silver kites dived over the long field where they'd be shooting off the fireworks later. And this really huge American flag was stretched across the back of a stage set up especially for the talent show. The first act had already started.

Not many people were sitting on the grass yet to watch. Some kid I didn't know danced around on the stage lip-synching a song I didn't want to know. He had on a black paper top hat and a thick black sweatshirt with a red bow tie pinned on it. He opened and shut his mouth like a fuzzy puppet.

"I've been looking all over for you, Hobart," this voice said next to my ear. Molly had seen me before I saw her. "You better hurry. The mayor's up now, and Miss Ivan-slow-witch is talking to Mr. Star, who's up right after the mayor."

The kid on the stage bowed with his mouth shut while his record went on singing the next song. "Up where?" I asked Molly.

"What do you mean, 'Where'? There!" she said, pointing to a crowd just across the baseball diamond. "Up on the dunk-tank seat. The mayor's been on it about ten minutes, and all the people from City Hall are throwing balls at three for fifty cents. They don't throw very straight, though, because they've only dropped her in the water twice."

From the dunk tank came a yell, a splash, and a lot of shouts and applause. "Well, three times."

Something seemed wrong again. Molly was still alone.

"Where's Lisa?" I asked her. "And Michelle? Are you mad at them or something?"

"She's talking to Mr. Star about *spooning*!"

"Lisa?"

"Of course not. Miss I've Got a Twitch. Do you know what spooning is?"

"Wait a minute. Let me get this straight. Lisa isn't talking to anybody, but Miss Ivanovitch is over at the dunk tank talking to Mr. Star about spooning?"

"Right. Spooning is this old-fashioned word for kissing." We both rolled our eyes. If I'd been a girl, she'd have made me give her a cootie shot. "I read it in a book," she went on. "You know, like billing and cooing and spooning."

"What are they saying about kissing?"

"I couldn't tell. But I don't like it. She's all wrong for him. Look, if you do dunk Mr. Star in that vat of water, he'll get so soaked they couldn't do any spooning today, at least. What do you think?"

"I thought balls would cost less," I told her. "Are they really fifty cents? That means I've only got enough money for six shots at him. Those Jay-cees must be minting money on that thing."

We started over to the tank just as somebody hit the target again and sent the mayor on another splashdown. The crowd clapped and whistled.

"Aren't you going to throw at him?" I asked Molly.

"At Mr. Star? You've got to be kidding."

The mayor climbed out of the tank onto the grass, looking like a wet cat. Somebody handed her a towel, and she wrapped it tightly around her shoulders.

"I'll give you money." Molly dug into her shorts pocket and pulled out a couple of dollar bills.

"Nothing doing," I told her. "If you want to dunk Mr. Star so bad, you've got to try too. He can't flunk us, you know." She rolled her eyes.

I had to get rid of Molly. Before long somebody was sure to see her with me and think I liked her. "Hey, look, there are the girls!" I yelled. Lisa, Michelle, and Jenny were hanging over the fence around the dunk tank. Boy, was I glad to see them. "I bet they're looking for you. Here she is!" I yelled, pointing with both hands. I gave her a little shove in their direction.

"Shhhh," Molly hissed, giving me a big shove back. "I'm not talking to them."

The girls saw us. I know they did. They turned away and started laughing like somebody was holding them down tickling their feet.

"Over here's where you pay." Molly tucked her head down and headed me off to buy tickets.

By the time we got in line, Mr. Star was easing himself onto the dunk-tank seat. He waved at us with his hands clamped over his head like he was a boxer. "You'll never get me," he yelled. "I'm feeling lucky." He had on jeans and an old Central School T-shirt, the kind of stuff he had worn when our class went once on Outdoor Education—stuff that didn't matter if it got dirty. Or wet.

He was sitting in this open-topped cage, like he was a monkey at the zoo. That way the balls wouldn't hit him if they flew out of the strike zone. Unless, of course, you threw a mountain curve that dropped in and bopped him on his bald spot.

To dunk him you had to hit a circle about eight inches across that tripped a lever that dropped the board he was sitting on. Then Mr. Star would splash into this four-foot-deep tank of water. It looked easy.

The crowd had thinned out. Most of the people had been there to soak the mayor. One guy said she'd been soaking *him* plenty with taxes. I guess even grown-ups like to make big guns look stupid. Not so many people knew Mr. Star, though, so the line for him was short. Rolf and his cousin Thor were first up.

Mr. Star didn't look scared or anything. He settled back on the seat and crossed his arms like he was watching any old ball game.

Across from us Miss Ivanovitch leaned on the fence on the other side of the dunk tank. She had on a red-and-white-striped dress and big blue star earrings. "I didn't know you two were good friends," she called, waving both hands at Molly and me.

I took one step away from Molly and she took one step away from me. The girl group, who were standing near Miss Ivanovitch, waved at us two-handed like she had, and then laughed until they doubled over. All except Lisa, who tossed her sausage curls and looked bored. The black stuff around her eyes was smudged and she still had some lipstick on her mouth, but she was dressed now in regular kid clothes.

"I'm just *standing* here," I said.

"It's a free country," Molly told Miss Ivanovitch, and the girls laughed some more.

Rolf wound up like a major-league pitcher and aimed at the target, which was about thirty feet away. The ball flew like a rocket straight across space, past the bull's-eye, *zap* into the net behind it.

Mr. Star grinned.

Rolf shrugged, wound up, and tried again. This time the ball wasn't so fast, but it landed in the net anyway.

Mr. Star laughed and linked his hands behind his head. The ball zipped wide once again, and Rolf stepped away from the line, grumbling.

His cousin wasn't any better. Threw three balls, missed three times, no problem. A couple of other kids tried, too, but Mr. Star stayed up on the seat high and dry.

"What's *in* that tank, Jack?" Miss Ivanovitch called to Mr. Star.

*"See?"* Molly hissed to me. "She called him *Jack*."

"That's not exactly a kiss," I told her.

"Piranhas, possibly," he said, "but at this rate I'll never know for sure."

I was next. "Have you been practicing?" Mr. Star asked, as I stood at the line loosening up my shoulders.

"I'm a hotshot," I told him. Toby in the fountain. Mr. Star in the dunk tank. This was going to be my day for cleaning up.

Molly didn't come to the line with me. Instead, she stood back like she didn't have anything to do with my being there. And when I wound up and let loose, she even yelled, "Jinx!" to make Mr. Star think she didn't want him zapped. So of course I missed.

That made me mad. I whirled around and pretended to throw the second ball at *her*, but I nearly dropped it instead. Standing next to her at the fence was Miss Ivanovitch.

Molly looked like she was the one caught in a cage. She was always telling kids how she didn't like Miss Ivanovitch. For sure now she'd have to give in and start talking to Lisa and the girls, if just to escape. But they hadn't circled around the dunk tank to join her like Miss Ivanovitch had. That's when I began to wonder if maybe they were the ones not talking to her.

"Hi, HO-bie," Michelle called. "Having a good time?"

"We're going to the state Miss Pre-Teen Personality Contest with Lisa this weekend," Jenny said. "Too bad Molly can't come." And the three of them headed toward the long line in front of the Moon Walk.

Molly crossed her arms and tossed her head, like she could care less. I turned away, took dead aim, and threw five more balls at Mr. Star's target. I hit the grass, the bees, the tank, the net, and a kid's leg. Mr. Star laughed. Each time. I didn't know whether that should get me an F in pitching or an A in kindness to teachers.

Mr. Star was swinging his legs back and forth now, feeling at home. "Only three more minutes in the hot seat!" he called out, glancing down at his watch. I wondered if it was waterproof. "Any more takers out there? The money goes to a good cause! The Jaycees are burying a Stockton time capsule on our good town's anniversary next Wednesday. Make a big splash and help them pay for it." Then he turned to me. "You're still planning to be there, aren't you, Hobie?"

"I guess," I told him.

"Me too," Molly said. "I wouldn't miss it. It's historic."

"Excellent," Mr. Star said. "Gold stars to you both. OK, step right up, folks! Three balls for fifty cents!" Molly didn't move.

I didn't have any more money. Well, a quarter, but that wasn't enough. Nobody was in line behind me. The talent show had started, and a one-man band on the stage had drawn away the dunk-tank crowd. Somebody's grandfather was playing the harmonica, banging on cymbals with a foot pedal, and scraping at an old washboard that hung around his neck like a bib. There was a horn that he squeezed every once in a while, and a bike bell that he rang. The crowd clapped along like it was great. I think he was playing "Oh, beautiful for spacious skies."

When I left the ball-throwing line, Mr. Star called, "Better luck next time, Hobie." And then he kind of blinked as he looked past me. I turned and blinked too. Stepping up to the mark, three balls in her hand, was Miss Ivanovitch.

And Molly had disappeared.

"Are you going to *throw* those?" I asked Miss Ivanovitch.

"I was thinking about it," she said, grinning at Mr. Star. She tossed one up and caught it, testing its weight. Putting her hand behind her about waist high, she turned the ball around and around in her fingertips, and then slammed it, *splat,* square into the center of the target.

Mr. Star held his hands out toward the cage wire, his eyes and his mouth wide open. He must have swallowed a mouthful.

"Remember, it's for a good cause," Miss Ivanovitch called to him as he climbed back onto the seat.

And nobody was there to see. Not a single kid I knew was still watching. I was the only one clapping like crazy.

"In college," Miss Ivanovitch began as she wound up again, "I was on the softball team." Not skipping a beat, she threw, hit *splat,* and dumped him once again into the tank. "We weren't half bad," she went on, while Mr. Star crawled up again, a little slower this time. "Look, Jack," she said, "I

don't have to throw this last ball. Just because I paid the money . . ."

"No, no," he told her. "Oh, no, that's . . . quite all right. Really. I wouldn't have volunteered to do this if I minded getting a little wet." He tilted his head and pounded it to empty the water out of his ear. "But, look, Svetlana, don't you have an appointment?"

"Not until two." And she didn't even give him time to hold his nose before she slammed the bull's-eye again. "We won the north division softball title my senior year," she went on like nothing special was happening and they were just having this normal conversation. "I pitched." She looked proud. He looked like a guppy.

If only Molly could have seen it. Those two wouldn't be spooning anytime soon, for sure. I couldn't tell if Mr. Star was mad or not. I would've been. Three times in the drink. Three out of three. I think she was showing off. But the thing about Miss Ivanovitch is, she's never dull.

The next name on the dunker list was the junior-high-school principal. He was jogging in place, wearing red-white-and-blue swimming trunks; but judging by the size of those kids waiting for him, I thought he should have brought scuba gear.

"Hobie? Hobie, look at me!" Toby's voice carried

through all the noise. He'd let loose of his pony's saddle to wave. I waved back. Eight hot ponies loped, heads down, around and around the bases of the ball diamond. With little kids on their backs, they made home run after home run, stopping now and then to dump on the track.

"Hobart! Hobart!" This time it wasn't Toby. Molly was calling from near the front of the Moon Walk line. The Moon Walk isn't exactly a ride. It's more of a jump—a huge, room-sized pillow of air covered with a tent of mesh so you can see the kids inside bouncing and flipping and knocking heads. It's fun.

"I had to leave," she called. "Did anybody get him?"

"You're not going to believe this," I yelled. I could hardly wait to tell her. "Miss Ivanovitch did it! She nearly drowned him. Three times!"

"You're kidding! Come *tell* me!" She was actually jumping up and down. "I've saved you a place. *Are* you kidding?"

I just wanted to tell her. I didn't want to stand in a line with her. I looked around to see if there was somebody else to cut in with, but there wasn't. So I went. And I gave her a blow-by-blow of the whole three-ball game. With sound effects.

"I told you she wasn't right for him," Molly

90

said. "I read Ann Landers. You've got to be nice. And that wasn't nice. Here," she went on, smiling, "I bought you a Moon Walk ticket. It cost fifty cents." She held it out, and I was just about to say, "Forget it," when she smiled even brighter and said, "Happy birthday."

When somebody gives you a birthday present, you can't very well say, "No, thank you." Even Ann Landers would tell you that. Maybe this is another Tom Sawyer thing happening, I thought, trying to remember the list. Anyway, I'd thrown practically all my money away on Mr. Star, and that was partly Molly's fault. Besides, I like jumping in the marshmallowy Moon Walk. I took the ticket.

The guy at the door blew his whistle, and the kids inside slowly stopped flinging themselves around and slid out. One of them ran over to the bushes and got sick.

When we're finished here, I decided, I'll lose Molly. I'll go find somebody to be in the pie-eating contest with me at three o'clock. Maybe the kid who got sick would be really hungry by then. We took our shoes off, crawled through the door flap onto this squooshy balloon, and started flipping and diving and flat-falling into humps that shook like chocolate pudding. Molly got a lot of kids singing

"Happy Birthday to You," and kids were jumping right next to me, bouncing me high. Then she pushed me over and I pushed her over. All in all, it wasn't a bad present.

When the man whistled, though, and we fell out the door onto the grass, I was glad I hadn't eaten the cotton candy.

Across the infield the talent-show speaker shrieked, crackled, and finally popped clear with "The next act, after those splendid Greene Brothers, Jim and Doug, with their wicked rhythm and blues— weren't they terrific, folks—is, well, it's a real novelty."

I ran off to see, leaving Molly to search for her sandals in the pile of shoes outside the Moon Walk.

"First time *I've* heard of such a thing," the announcer went on. "It's a performance by one of our very own Central School teachers."

No matter how hard I tried, I couldn't work my way very far toward the front of the crowd that was sitting, standing, and lying on the grass in front of the makeshift stage. Off to the side I could see Mr. Star, who'd changed his clothes somewhere, and I wondered if he was going to do a stand-up comic act using some of his old 4B jokes.

"Yes, ladies and gentlemen, boys and girls," the announcer went on, "to delight . . . and astonish . . . you all at this joyful Fourth of July celebration"—he held his arms out to the side of the stage—"here is our very own charming, talented, new fifth-grade teacher . . . Miss Svetlana Ivanovitch! Did I pronounce that OK?"

And that's who it was, all right, running out onto the stage in her red-white-and-blues. She sat down on a folding chair and, after pulling the microphone down low, took two shining metal things out of her skirt pocket. She tucked them between the fingers of her right hand, which she had curled into a fist. Then she started to rattle the things back and forth, hitting one against the palm of her left hand and the other against her knee and both of them against each other so fast you could hardly see what was happening. But you could hear. It was a clicking, tinny, snappy sound, like castanets.

The old man who'd played the washboard and bicycle bell whooped and clapped from the audience. Other people clapped too. The clicking got faster and snappier like a drum solo in a jazz band. And then, clicking them only a little to keep time, Miss Ivanovitch sang "My country, 'tis of thee." She had a high voice that didn't sound all that bad. The old man sang with her for "Of thee I sing."

I looked everywhere for Molly. She was missing the best part of the day. Without looking embarrassed at all, in front of everybody, with people clapping along and singing, Miss Ivanovitch was playing a pair of old tablespoons. To delight and astonish us all, as the guy said. She was spooning. In public.

# 8

# Give Him a Kiss, Sweetheart!

On the crowded park sidewalk, a kid was lighting snakes. Not rattlers or cobras or anything. We don't get them much in our park. These look like tiny hockey pucks. You put a match to one, and blackish ash crawls out the top, wiggling and squirming, till it's about a foot long—unless you get a dud. This kid's weren't duds.

He was skinny, with yellow-white hair that hung over his eyes, and he was wearing a big blue ribbon on his T-shirt. Lots of kids were wearing ribbons, because there were lots of contests to win—kite flying, sand-castle building, running. "What's the ribbon for?" I asked him, "Sack race or something?"

"Water-balloon toss," the kid told me, lighting another snake egg. It sputtered and started to grow. "First place." I'd seen an Explorer Scout earlier in the day dragging a huge plastic trash can filled with softball-sized water balloons, and I'd wanted to enter that contest, but I didn't have anybody to toss with. Nick and I almost won two years ago.

"Who'd you throw to?" I asked him. If he didn't

have somebody regular, maybe he could be in the pie-eating contest with me.

"My mother," he said. The snake grew out about two inches before it fizzed and stopped.

"Your mother!"

"She's good at it." He poked the snake with a stick.

Throwing water balloons with his mother! This guy needed me even more than I needed him. "I just thought maybe you might be my partner in the pie-eating contest. I mean, they do it by age groups, so you couldn't enter with your mother. Even if she wanted to."

"She's playing bingo now." He stepped on the sick snake and snuffed it out.

"I'd be in the ten-to-twelve group," I told him. I mean, I'd been ten to twelve for almost a whole day.

"I just turned eight," he said, and picking up a small brown bag, he started to walk away.

"They'll never know how old you are. How could they find out?" I followed him. He might be my only chance. "You're tall. And I can show you how it's done," I told him. "Give you a few tips. I know all about pie-eating. You'd get another blue ribbon."

He stopped. "What kind of pie?"

"I don't know. Pie."

After chewing awhile on his bottom lip, he said, "Well, OK, if you think it's all right. But only if it's not coconut cream. I wouldn't eat coconut cream pie for any color ribbon." He turned toward the bingo tent. "I'll go tell my mom."

"The contest starts at three," I said, making sure he had a watch on. "It's almost that now. I'll meet you at the pie truck at ten to."

He nodded.

"What's you name?" I called.

"Alex," he said, and he reached into his bag and tossed me a snake. I figured that meant he'd really be there.

Putting it in my pocket, I headed over to check things out at the contest field, where the balloon-sitting race was beginning. Toby was in it. It's for kids three to five who don't know any better. Their mothers blow up balloons, and the kids have to sit on them to see how fast they can break them while all the grown-ups laugh. I sure wouldn't want to do it. Mothers who know how to win blow the balloons up big so they explode easy. Mothers who are in a hurry, or don't have much air because they smoke, blow the balloons up a little, and the kid has to bounce like crazy before the thing finally goes *pow*.

Mrs. Rossi had been at it a few years, and I watched her huff and puff until she had a red balloon up to the size of a prize watermelon. She tied a fast knot and put it on the grass, and Toby sat down like he was afraid it would blast him into orbit. But all Mrs. Rossi had to do was push down a little bit on his shoulders and it was a goodbye balloon. Toby stopped crying almost as soon as they gave him a ribbon. Every kid in the Balloon Break got a ribbon and a little flag. They deserved it, too.

An Explorer Scout sat on the back of a truck guarding the pies. "What kind of pies are they?" I asked him.

"Cream," he told me, looking away.

"I know that. I mean what flavors?"

"We're not allowed to say. You take what I give you." This guy thought he was a Marine.

The pie boxes were stacked high in the truck, and I moved in closer to look at the labels. The Scout flicked on a bullhorn and pointed it at me. "Everybody back from the truck!" he blared. "*Away* from the truck!" And that drew kids like flies.

The seven—eight—nine-year-olds were first. They lined up in pairs, pushing and shoving, most of them with no idea how to win. They looked so young. I knew I could tell them a thing or two.

Almost three o'clock and no blond kid. I'd have run off to the bingo tent to get him, but I didn't want to lose my place in line. Marshall and Trevor were there, and Rolf and his cousin, and a few other guys I knew, but nobody else alone. Michelle and Jenny were in line, but not Lisa, who, I guess, didn't want to spoil her image. There's probably nothing that'll spoil your image like a cream pie in the face.

As the little kids took their pies and headed for the field, I moved in close and checked out the flavors: chocolate cream, banana cream, lemon, vanilla, cherry-berry cream. Coconut. Only a few flavor complaints, but the Scout held firm. I watched him dig his thumb into the pies as he handed them out, and then lick it when he got an inch or so built up. I don't think a Marine would have done that.

Dust from the pony circle drifted in over the contest field, which was sprinkled with bright-colored balloon bits. The kids carefully put the pie plates down on the grass and then searched for their folks, for *anybody,* to give them advice.

I decided to be nice and tell them how. "Smash your face in it!" I yelled. A couple of second graders looked over at me, then back at their pie, and then they just walked away, leaving even the swirls of whipped cream unlicked.

"OK," the Scout called into the bullhorn. "We've got three judges in the field. Wave your hands, judges, so everybody can see who you are. OK, here are the rules. You must eat the whole pie. No fair using your hands. Keep them behind you while you eat or you will be disqualified. When you're finished, stand up and show the empty plate to the judge nearest you. The first couple with a clean plate wins. Heads up! OK, ready, get set . . ." He looked around to make sure nobody was cheating, and then he blew his whistle.

The judges took over the contest, and the Scout turned to us. "OK, ten-to-twelve-year-olds, you're next." Kids started shoving each other and grabbing pies, and I lost my place in line ten times over. I was all ready to give up completely when I felt this tap on my shoulder. "Sorry I'm late. Are you ready?" Molly asked. "I'm *starved*."

Molly? Ready to enter a race with Molly Bosco? I'd never be able to go back to school. "I . . . I'm not hungry," I told her, looking all over for the kid with blond hair. "I ate a late lunch. Cotton candy. The Moon Walk. I'm not feeling good. Besides . . ."

And that's when Alex ran up, out of breath. "You still need me?" he asked.

"Yes," I sighed. "Yes, I need you," I told him. "Alex, wow, you're just in time. Look, Molly, I promised Alex I'd do the pie-eating thing with him. I just got my appetite back. Come on, Alex."

She cocked her head. "I've seen that kid somewhere before."

"He won the balloon toss," I explained, not telling her she'd probably seen him in the second-grade play. I guided him up to the Scout.

"Here you go!" The guy held out a pie. A mound of its filling was stuck to his thumb. The top of the pie was heaped with toasted coconut.

"Coconut doesn't like Alex," I said, not taking it. "It makes him throw up."

"You take what I give you, kid."

"You had your thumb in it, so it's got germs."

He licked him thumb. "Coconut's all I've got left."

Inside the truck were at least three more boxes of pies. He saw me looking at them. "Those are for the thirteen-to-fifteen group. Take the coconut or leave it."

"I hate coconut," Alex said.

"If you hold your breath you won't taste it," I told him.

"I love coconut," Molly said. "My favorite foods are coconut, catfish, and artichokes."

Didn't sound right to me. "What about stew?" I asked her. "I was sure that was your personal favorite."

"Last call for ten-to-twelves!" the Scout blasted on his bullhorn right next to my ear.

"Come on, Hobie," Molly said, taking the coconut cream pie. "I won't bite you."

I'd have to be crazy to do this, I thought. Or maybe I'd have to be crazy not to. After all, I'm an expert. I know how to win. And I only get one chance a year. They don't have a pie-eating race on Field Day at school. Or any other day. Just on the Fourth of July.

"Listen, Alex, I'm really sorry," I told him, "but I think maybe she's got a bigger mouth than you do. And besides, it's coconut, and, you know . . ." Alex nodded and shrugged his shoulders.

I followed Molly. She chose a spot at the side of the field, not too messy from the little kids. So that's where I got down on my knees, locked my hands behind me, and faced Molly Bosco and a coconut cream pie with a thumb hole in it.

"Listen," I said fast, while the guy was explaining the rules. "First, take a good deep breath. Then eat as much as you can, and when you come up for air, I'll take over. OK? Get as much of the pie on your face and in your hair as you can. Pie that gets on your face and in your hair you don't have to eat. Got it?"

She didn't get it. When the whistle blew, Molly was still staring at me, holding the hair back from her face. So I started first. I smooshed my head back and forth across the pie, ate two gigantic bites, and then raised up so she could take over. It wasn't bad. A little pasty, but not bad.

Molly carefully lowered her head and stuck her tongue out a little toward the cream at the edge of the crust. She'd said she wouldn't bite me, and she didn't, but she wasn't biting the pie, either! I couldn't believe it! If I was going to risk permanent embarrassment by eating a coconut cream pie with Molly Bosco, I was at least going to win some kind of prize for it.

So I put my hand very gently on the back of her head and shoved her face into the pie as hard as I could. If Mrs. Rossi could help Toby along by giving him a little push, why couldn't I help Molly? She didn't know it was coming, though, so she yelped and flicked her head to the side. The flick smashed half the pie out onto the grass. A spectacular move. I wished I'd thought of it myself. Pie on the grass you don't have to eat either.

When she raised up, howling, I took a deep breath and attacked what was left with my mouth wide open. And I was just about to swallow a huge chunk when something caught the back of my head like a hammer. Molly Bosco had smashed me into the goo. I sucked in my breath, and got wads of whipping cream up both sides of my nose, and swept my head to the side to get free. That pushed another mess of pie onto the grass. Gasping, I looked down at the plate through clogged eyelashes and saw that there wasn't a crumb left. But it was Molly who grabbed the empty pie plate, stood up waving it back and forth, and yelled, "First!"

I had won. Almost fair and square. Molly, too.

Michelle looked up at us. I think it was Michelle. "Ooo-oosick," she said, wiping her fingers on the grass. "Do you know how totally *gross* you look?" From what I could tell, she and Jenny hadn't even started eating yet. Maybe they were waiting for forks.

Nobody else was standing up. Nobody was even close. So we made our way around all the picky eaters to the exit, where the lady who was in charge of pinning on ribbons was also handing out paper towels. She gave Molly and me one blue ribbon and two towels each.

"Wait!" a guy called, as we took the towels. "Don't rub the stuff off yet. Hold it." My eyes were mostly creamed together, so I couldn't see him too clearly. "I've got to get this. You're perfect. Exactly what I'm looking for. Just stand still and smile." I smiled.

I wondered if Molly had smiled. After all, I'd given her a pretty big shove. Then, prying my eyelashes apart, I looked at her and saw what Michelle had been talking about. Molly did look gross. Whipped cream, coconut, and chunks of crust hung off her nose, her chin, and her eyebrows. "Are you mad?" I asked her. I hoped she wasn't bleeding under all that.

"We won, didn't we?" she said. "You know, you look disgusting. Did I kill you?"

"Of course not," I lied. My nose was going to be flat forever.

"OK, kids," the man said, "it's fabulous with the pie all over your faces, but something's missing. You know? It just doesn't tell the story. I need a picture that says, 'Golly, we won!' You know?"

Picture? This guy was taking our *picture*. He had a camera!

"I tell you what," he went on. "Give him a kiss, sweetheart. Just a peck. Hold it. Fabulous."

I didn't even see it coming. I didn't have a chance to duck. She *kissed* me. Molly kissed me. On the cheek. On purpose.

Actually, I didn't feel a thing. I mean, she didn't actually kiss *me*. She kissed the coconut cream. As soon as I realized what she'd done, though, my face got hot enough to bake the pie. This was crazy, really crazy. Miss Ivanovitch wasn't the only one. I'd been spooning, too. In public. For real.

"Let me get your names," the photographer said, but I got out of there fast. My mouth wasn't working, but my legs sure were.

Molly hit the water fountain just after I did. I'd

turned it on as high as it would go and stuck my right cheek over it to wash away the kiss. Molly held her face in the water and then put her thumb over the spray and squirted me. I mean, it wasn't really funny, it was awful, but still we were laughing so hard that for a minute it was almost as crazy as being with Nick.

All that water and two paper towels each didn't do us much good. She looked like a scarecrow, so I guess I did, too. What we needed was the dunk tank.

But then, when I thought about what had happened, I stopped laughing right away.

"What did you have to do *that* for?" I asked her. "That was really stupid."

"Do what?" she asked, digging whipped cream out of her ear.

"What do you mean, 'Do what?' You know . . . what that guy said." My face turned red again. I could feel the heat crawl up my neck.

She shrugged her shoulders. "Don't think I *wanted* to do it. I just did what he told me to."

"If he told you to jump into the lake, would you do that?"

"You sound like my grandmother." She wiped her hands on her shorts. "Anyway, you tasted disgusting."

"I tasted like coconut cream pie." Alex was headed toward us with this woman and another little kid. "Who was that man taking pictures?" I asked Molly.

"How should I know?"

The woman with Alex smiled at us, showing braces on her teeth. "This is my mother," Alex said. "We watched you eat, and she wants to meet you."

"Marietta Glass," she told us, shaking our gummy hands. "Congratulations . . . I think. You were really something. But that's one blue ribbon I'm glad we didn't go for." She looked us over and smiled like she thought we were pretty funny. "I did win a big prize, though," and she pointed down at the little kid, not Alex, who was carrying a stuffed giraffe as tall as he was. "Playing bingo," she explained. "Show them, Chuckie."

The kid shifted the giraffe behind him, away from the goo monsters.

"I think I won today because I'm wearing my good-luck pin." On her shoulder was a silver bird with a wingspan about an inch long. It had a tiny yellow eye that was shining as if there was a light behind it. "The pin was my great-grandmother's," she said. "The eye is a diamond. It was lucky even for her."

"We didn't need luck," Molly said.

"You certainly were amazing," Mrs. Glass went on. "It didn't look like fun. Was it?"

"Not much," I told her.

"Yes, it was," Molly lied. "And the pie was excellent."

"Well, you were terrific." Mrs. Glass grinned. "Look, we've got to go," she said, "but as a mother type, I expect I should tell you." She shook her head. "Your ribbons are running, and it may not come out in the wash."

"If they have a popcorn-eating contest, let me know," Alex said. And the three of them plus giraffe hurried off toward the bingo tent.

I looked at Molly. I'd never seen her with her hair messed up or with grass stains on her knees before. Usually she looked like she'd just had a shower and put on ironed clothes. Now not only was her whole head sticky, but little blue rivers were running down her shirt.

About six feet away, almost behind a tree, Michelle and Jenny were standing, watching us. They weren't wearing any ribbons, and their faces were clean.

"We *saw* what happened over there," Michelle sang. Molly smiled. I got a drink of water.

"She kissed you!" Jenny told me.

"I know it," Molly said, like they were talking

to her. She tossed her head, trying to flip her hair, but it was too stiff to move.

The girls came closer. I backed away. "The man told her to," I explained.

"If he'd told her to jump in the lake, would she do that?" Lisa asked, and I rolled my eyes.

"Jenny and I are going to the fireworks with Lisa tonight," Michelle said to no one in particular.

Molly lifted her chin. "How nice. You can watch Lisa's little curls hop up and down. You could all sit with us," she said, "but I only have enough sparklers for two." She looked at me and smiled.

Sparklers for two.

"You and *Hobie?*" Michelle asked, like no cootie shot could cure that. Molly nodded.

I didn't wait a minute. Not even a second. I whirled around and ran straight home like a string of firecrackers was shooting off at my heels.

Eating pie was one thing. But nobody—not even for one day—*nobody* was going to turn me into Molly Bosco's boyfriend.

# 9

# Like a Dandelion in the Sky

My pillow was so soft. After I'd showered off the pie glue, I just put my wet head on it for a few minutes. Well, maybe more than a few. Taking a nap is little-kid stuff, but boy, was I knocked out.

When I woke up the second time on my birthday, it felt funny, like getting older twice in one day. I blinked awhile trying to remember the first half of being ten. I'd kissed a girl, like Tom Sawyer did. Sort of. Somehow the Tom Sawyer things weren't turning out the same for me.

I walked around the house rubbing my eyes and calling to find out who was home. Nobody was, but my mom had left me a note on the kitchen table. "Sorry we missed you. We're having a picnic with the Rossis. Meet us at six o'clock on the big field where we always watch fireworks. Bring a flashlight. I have fried chicken and potato salad. Also look for a big chocolate-chip cake with eleven candles. One to grow on. See you at six. Love, Mom." It was already seven.

I grabbed a flashlight and some matches, slammed

the kitchen door, and put the snake puck that Alex had given me on the back steps. It lit easy, and the snake, fat as my little finger, squirmed out and headed off the top step like it thought it was a Slinky.

The streets going to the park were packed with cars and buses bringing people to the band concert and the fireworks show. At the entrance, Explorer Scouts stood around tents with red crosses on the sides waiting, I guess, for people to faint.

Finding my folks wasn't going to be all that easy. It wasn't dark yet, so the flashlight wouldn't help me spot them. All the way down to the lake where the fireworks would be was practically a rug of picnickers. The only hole in the rug was behind the huge maple tree, because if you sat there, the tree blocked your view of the sky. From a little hill near the water came the sound of the high school band playing "I'm a Yankee Doodle Dandy," and old people here and there were singing along. A kindergarten girl waved this little flag she'd probably won sitting on balloons.

I leaped over and around red-checked tablecloths, kids wrestling, a baby spread with mosquito netting, people lying on their stomachs playing magnetic Scrabble. No Mom and Dad. No Rossis. Not even Toby. I ducked a Frisbee and told Mrs. Glass I was sorry I couldn't stay for sandwiches with Alex and Chuckie because it was my birthday. She recognized me even without my pie face on.

And then I spotted my folks. They were just in front of the tree. Actually Dad saw me first and yelled. He was pointing to an old bicycle flag next to him. They'd gotten it years ago when my bike had training wheels and they thought a flag would keep me from getting squashed. Fastened to it was a cardboard sign shaped like a birthday cake. When I got closer, I could see red, white, and blue paper candles on the cake. And then, finally, I made out the lettering on the side in brown ballpoint pen and glued-down chocolate chips. !!!HOBIE!!! it said.

Oh, no, I thought. They're having a surprise party for me. My mom had asked all these kids and they'd been hiding out someplace for an hour and a half ready to pop up and say, "Surprise!" And she was going to want us to play Pin the Fuse on the Firecracker like we did when I was eight.

I was wrong, though. The flag was there just so I'd find them. It wasn't a party at all. But it sure was a surprise.

Sitting with my folks on two old quilts were Mr. and Mrs. Rossi and Toby, who was curled up asleep, his thumb in his mouth. *And,* on a big plaid blanket in the middle of them all, were Mrs. Bosco—and Molly. Actually, Mrs. Bosco, who is very big, took up most of their blanket, so Molly was sitting on a corner of ours. In the middle of our quilt was a real chocolate-chip cake with eleven candles on it.

I sank down next to my mom. "What's going *on?*" I asked her.

"Aren't you glad they're having fireworks again, just for your birthday!" she said brightly. It was this big joke that when I was little I thought the fireworks were for me. Nobody laughed. She lowered her voice. "You're extremely late."

"I fell asleep," I whispered. And so of course she had to say it out loud to the whole field of people. "Imagine *that*! The birthday boy took a nap!"

But I was too hungry to be mad. I could have beaten a bear at a drumstick-and-potato-salad-eating contest. Absolutely fair and square. Without smearing any on my face and hair.

Before I munched the last bone clean, though, I closed my eyes, made a wish, and blew out the candles so everybody else could start on the birthday cake. I wished for Nick to be home so things could be just like they were before, but when I opened my eyes, they weren't.

Anyway, I got all the cake that was left on the plate, and I got the plate, too, with its big ring of frosting. As I ran my finger around it, my mom whispered to me behind her hand, "Mrs. Bosco and Molly were here all by themselves, and what with Molly's parents being in Pakistan, Molly seemed very lonely. So when they asked us to join them, I said certainly. You don't mind, do you?"

"Yes," I told her. "I mind."

Molly smiled at me. She'd washed her hair too, and all the coconut was off her neck, but she had the faded blue pie ribbon pinned on a clean yellow shirt. I'd left my ribbon at home. That pie-eating contest had gotten me into enough trouble already.

"You be nice to Molly," Mom told me. "Do you hear, Hobie? She's a sweet girl."

"She's a *girl*," I said, planning to stay as far away from Molly Bosco as possible.

"What's wrong with girls?" Mom asked. I rolled my eyes.

"Hey, sleepyhead, we got a letter from Nick yesterday," Mr. Rossi called across the blankets. "He wrote it on a computer that corrects spelling, and every word was right. How about that! He's doing a project that involves grasshopper research. And he says he has a neat roommate. He works out every afternoon rowing on the lake." Mr. Rossi smiled broadly and took another bite of cake. "So how's *your* summer going, Tom Sawyer? Doing anything? Learning anything? Moving the ball down the court?"

"Leave the kid alone," my dad called to him. "He's on vacation. He doesn't have to score points."

Molly narrowed her eyes at Mr. Rossi. "Hobie's going to City Hall on Wednesday," she told him. "He's going to be an official person at the Stockton Anniversary Time Capsule Ceremony."

"That's my kid," Dad said. My folks thought it was great that I was representing my class. I didn't tell them I was the only one who had volunteered.

Mr. Rossi kind of snorted.

I wasn't sure what to say. So I ate another fingerful of chocolate frosting and smiled a sticky smile.

"Hobie won a blue ribbon today too," Molly told Mr. Rossi.

"No kidding!" My dad turned around from talking to Mrs. Bosco. "That's the way to go. For what? Three-legged race? Who'd you run with?"

I choked on the frosting and couldn't answer.

"Grandmother"—Molly stood up—"can we light the sparklers now?"

I stood up too. Fast. I wasn't about to admit pie eating with Molly Bosco. I couldn't tell if she had saved me on purpose. That would have been nice. Molly isn't famous for being nice.

My dad lit the first sparkler, and Molly drew *O*'s and stars with it in the almost dark. I lit mine from hers and made a figure 8 and then, drawing lots of them, said, "Eight times eight is . . ."

"Sixty-four," Molly whispered.

"Sixty-four!" I said, loud, to let Mr. Rossi know I knew more than a thing or two. The air smelled totally sparkler. Nothing else smells like that.

We'd just finished off the whole box of sparklers when the first explosion came. Somebody screamed, and then all at once the whole crowd was yelling. A rocket shot up and lit a thousand green fountains. Each spark broke into millions of drops, and they all rained into the lake. The screams lasted until the lights died out. It made our sparklers look like nothing.

After a minute or two of black, another rocket exploded like a giant sneeze in the sky, white and silver when it popped and then orange and gold on the way down.

"Wow," "Fabulous," "Ohhhhhhhh," people went, and clapped, like the fireworks could hear them and feel proud.

Toby's dad woke him up to watch, but he cried and wouldn't look. It must have been almost as scary as sitting on a balloon.

Molly leaned over. "Close your eyes tight right after it explodes, and you'll see it again."

I did and she was right. Except the colors are different with your eyes shut.

For about ten minutes more the fireworks went off—sometimes three, four at a time—pounding away, *pow-pow-pow-BAM*. The noise hit houses and trees and bounced back at us. And the ground under the quilt shook so you could feel it all the way up to your nose. Then they lit all they had left—about a dozen at once, with hundreds of green and red dandelions and silver and gold octopus legs dissolving into tiny bits.

And then it stopped.

"Is that all?" somebody asked. "Is it over?" I don't know what more they wanted.

"Look at that!" Toby called, pointing behind us.

"Oh, that's just the moon," his dad told him. "That's up there every night."

It looked like a very thin slice of melon and wasn't shedding much light on the crowd.

Even if you couldn't see all the people too well, you could hear them and feel them. They were gathering up and moving out toward the street.

"Will somebody carry these pillows?"

"Where's the basket?"

"Is Eli with you?"

"Did anybody bring a flashlight?"

I turned mine on and pointed it across the field, where everybody seemed to be shaking out blankets and folding them.

"Is that Miss Ivanovitch?" I asked Molly, showing her with my flashlight beam. "And Mr. Star?"

"Where? Here? Tonight? You're kidding," she said.

"There. The ones folding up a blanket."

"*Which* ones?"

"Where are you?" a woman called. "Don't be lost!"

"Over there," I told her. "Maybe it was just people who looked like them." I shrugged. "You can ask Mr. Star when school starts."

"Chuckie!" the voice called, closer.

"If it's not too late by then," Molly said.

"*Chuckie!* Where are you?" It was Mrs. Glass shouting. And then she spotted Molly. "Have you seen Chuckie? The one with the giraffe, only he doesn't have it now? Remember him? Did he come this way?"

"I didn't see him."

"He may have been crying," she said.

"Me either," I told her.

Kids were everywhere, a lot of them crying because it was past their bedtime and it was dark and there were probably monsters.

"Can we help?" Dad asked.

"This is Mrs. Glass," I told him.

"Oh, please do," she said. "I've got this real problem. Alex is staked out where we had our picnic, because I lost my pin there, my great-grandmother's pin. *You* know what it looks like." She pointed at me. "I had my nose in the grass searching for the pin, and then I saw that Chuckie was gone."

"Your lucky pin?" Molly asked.

"Could you look for it while Alex and I find Chuckie? Please. I'll show you where. CHUCKIE!" she shouted, but nobody answered.

"Sure. I've got a flashlight. Look, I'll see you guys at home," I told my dad, who nodded.

"Mrs. Glass," he said, "I'll walk the other way and call your son's name. If I find him, I'll bring him to the first-aid tent."

She ran, and I followed with my flashlight bobbing.

"Alex!" she yelled, and this time there was an answer.

"Nobody could have stolen him, could they?" she asked me. "Chuckie's so cute, everybody wants to hug him. I had them both fingerprinted and their pictures taken last winter, but Chuckie's grown so." And she looked like she wanted to run all directions at once. "The pin doesn't matter. I mean, it matters, but it doesn't *really* matter. It should be right where Alex is. You didn't move, did you Alex?"

"Not much," he said. An NFL bedspread was draped over his shoulder.

She grabbed his hand and they started off, yelling, "Chuckie!" together.

# 10

# Bump in the Night

I was afraid to crouch down and start looking. Even with the flashlight on, somebody might trip over me. Hundreds of people, maybe thousands, their eyes blocked with picnic stuff, were headed toward home and bed. And toward me. They weren't looking where they were walking much.

"Chuckie . . ." Mrs. Glass had a voice that carried.

I stood and aimed the beam around people's ankles as they pushed past. Something glittered in the grass.

"Look, I'll hold the light, and you feel around in the dirt," Molly said, grabbing the flashlight from my hand. "I told my grandmother I'd be home in half an hour."

At first I was mad. I mean, why did she have to be there bossing me around? This was *my* job. She was always butting in. But then, Molly or not, I felt a whole lot better knowing some guy with a picnic hamper wasn't going to step on my head while I was on my hands and knees.

"Hey, I found . . ."

"Already?" Molly asked.

". . . a quarter," I told her. That's what had been shining. I put it in my pocket.

"There's a pile of chicken bones by your feet," she said, turning the light away. "And some used sparklers."

Crawling in a circle feeling the grass, I found a dime and half a Snickers bar. The ants had found it before I did, and they were climbing all over their chocolate-nut mountain. Mr. Star used to tell us we'd be amazed at what lived in a cubic yard of dirt. I was pretty surprised at what was just living on top of it.

"Let me try." Molly handed me the flashlight, and I played floor lamp while she crawled. Before long she'd come up with a couple of pennies, three empty Coke cans, and a Gumby watch with a broken strap, but no bird pin.

"Listen," I told her, "in case I don't find it tonight, I'd better mark this spot so I'll know where to look in the morning. This is just open field. Piling up Coke cans wouldn't do it. Those are everywhere." Then I remembered how I'd been able to find my folks earlier. I looked over my shoulder, and even in the dark I could see it. They'd left the Hobie cake behind. It was tilting near the big old tree.

I tossed Molly the flashlight. "Don't move," I

told her, and started for the flag. Traffic was slowing down some, but I was heading the wrong way, against the flow of baby buggies and high-school kids with their arms linked six across.

When I finally grabbed the long plastic pole, I felt like a mountain climber who'd just reached the top of the peak. I yanked it out and there, right at the base, was the spoon that had been in Mom's potato salad. But when I leaned over to pick it up, this huge guy ran into me and flattened me on the ground. Me, the spoon, and the pole. I had to roll over and up fast so he wouldn't step on my stomach, too. He didn't even say he was sorry. He was dragging a kid about five years old, who was screaming.

"Chuckie!" I called. I mean, what if it was him? "Is that Chuckie?" I asked, stepping in front of the man.

"It's Owen," the guy told me, scooping the kid up and hurrying off.

"Chuckie?" I called, louder.

"What?" a small voice answered from somewhere behind me.

"Is that you?" I asked it.

"Who?" There was a pause. "My mother won't let me talk to strangers."

I still didn't see him, but I followed the sound to the big tree and circled it. On the side away from the lake, there he was, with his head against a fat root like it was a pillow.

"You know me," I told him. "I saw you today after you won the giraffe."

"I didn't win it. My mom did." He rubbed his eyes.

"She's looking for you."

"Where is she?" He blinked at the dark, not seeming scared at all. Probably he'd been asleep and didn't even know he was lost. "Did she find the lucky bird? I was looking for it, but I got tired."

"We'll go see," I said, taking his hand and pulling him to his feet. As we walked toward Molly, I called out, loud, "Mrs. Glass!"

"Mommy!" he yelled.

"That won't do you any good," I explained. "Half the women out here are called that." A few of them had even turned around.

"Hobie, I found a nail clipper in the—" Molly said when she saw me. Then she flashed the light at the kid. "Who's that?"

I grabbed his hand, figuring he might bolt when he found out his mother wasn't there. "It's the one, the only, the giraffe-high Chuckie Glass. He was out looking for the lucky pin and sat down under a tree to rest."

"Where's my mommy?" he asked Molly. And

then, pointing down at the pool of light where the flashlight beamed, said, "There's her bird. Where is she?"

Molly yelped. Me too. I dropped the flag and dived for the silver bird, whose eye blinked yellow.

The kid was calm, though. "That must be where she dropped it," he said. And you couldn't argue with that.

I fastened the pin on his shirt. "She'll be glad you were the one who found it," I told him.

"OK, where is she?" he asked, like we had her hidden someplace.

"I think," Molly said, "she's at the first-aid tent."

"Did she cut herself?" He was starting to get scared now, or mad. He shook free of my hand and broke away running.

"She's fine." Molly grabbed him by the collar and aimed him at the park entrance.

"Mommy!" he called on the run.

"Mrs. Glass!" Molly and I yelled over and over as we dashed after him. And that did it. With Alex beside her, Mrs. Glass appeared out of the dark from the direction of the first-aid tent, arms open wide. She scooped Chuckie up, and they both started bawling. It was embarrassing.

After I'd explained that nobody had stolen him and Molly had told her about how he was the one

who found the pin, Mrs. Glass opened her purse and tried to pay us.

"Look, I only have a dollar and thirty-four cents with me," she said, counting it out in her hand, "but I have more at home."

"Oh, no thanks," I said. "That's OK."

"But you found my treasures. Chuckie and the pin, too." Chuckie clung to her neck, knowing now that he'd been lost.

"We've already got paid," Molly said, showing her some of the stuff we'd found.

"And lots more," I told her. "There's money and . . . spoons and, you know, all over the field. It must fall out of people's pockets when they look up at the fireworks. And off blankets when they shake them."

"Hobie and I are going out tomorrow morning. We're going to search for more," Molly told her.

"What is this 'we' stuff?" I asked Molly.

"We may get rich because of you," she went on, like I hadn't said anything. "Already we have enough to buy two purple Popsicles."

"Well," Mrs. Glass said, "you two earned another ribbon each, but I don't have any for rescuers. I'll think of something special. I promise." She had Alex write our names on a little pad, and then they trudged off home.

So did I. Molly headed off with a family that lived on her street. "See you early," she called. I'd already decided *I* was going out early. Maybe, I thought, if I set my birthday-present alarm clock and got up at four o'clock or even five, I'd miss her.

I was really tired, so I set it for six.

# 11

# Snake in the Grass

I got there at seven.

"Here it is! I found it!" Molly yelled, as soon as she saw me across the field.

"Found what?" I called back, looking to see if there were any kids around from school who'd know us. There weren't, so I went over to where she was.

"I found what we're putting in the time capsule. It was under a tree next to a bunch of picnic stuff." And she started to laugh. "When they take it out of the time capsule, those future people will know *exactly* what we're like."

"What do you mean, we?" I asked. "You're the one who's adding it, not me."

Molly had beat me to the park by long enough to collect a batch of things in the big grocery sack she'd brought with her.

"Look at this," she said, opening the sack. I could make out a pair of sunglasses, a cassette tape, one big blue heart earring, a batch of change, and a scrunched-up brown lunch bag.

"What's in there?" I asked, poking the lunch bag.

"That's our time capsule thing."

"*Your* time capsule thing."

"Ours."

I shrugged. "Is it really good?"

"You're not going to believe it!" And she started to laugh again.

"Well, let's see."

"I thought you said it was mine." She took the whole grocery sack away and held it behind her back. The money in it jingled.

We weren't the only ones in the park. A man and a woman with metal detectors and earphones were sweeping the grass fast, like they'd done it a million times before. When their ears buzzed on something they couldn't see, they'd dig a hole to find the buried treasure.

"You really think you're going to put something extra in the capsule on Wednesday?" I asked her. "I mean, you think the Jaycees will let you? What is it, anyway?"

She smiled mysteriously, picked up a worn yellow baby blanket, and dropped it into the sack. "Oh, I'll just tell them it's important. Besides, it's small."

I tried guessing, but she wouldn't tell. So I just

cruised the field, picking up dimes and pennies, a couple of Go Bot robots, and an empty saltshaker. By nine o'clock we had a bag almost as full and almost as junky as our bags on locker-clean-out day.

That's when I had to cut out for the Rossis' house. Toby was probably sitting on the front steps waiting for the next exciting installment of the big alphabet mystery. What comes after H-I-J-K? I thought Molly would stick around in the park scrounging for more money and yellow diamonds, but instead she grabbed the bag of stuff and followed me.

"We're not going to get much more," she said, pointing at the street. "The park cleanup crew is here." And sure enough, a bunch of guys were jumping off trucks, emptying trash cans, and spiking potato-chip bags with pointed sticks.

"Well, OK, see you sometime," I told her. "Maybe we can decide what to do with our treasures." Treasures. I had to laugh at that. Except for the money, most of the stuff we'd found wasn't any good to anybody but the people who'd lost it.

I started to run. Sometimes Mrs. Rossi had places to go while I was with Toby, and she didn't like it much when I was late.

"Wait up," Molly called, and I slowed down a little. "Listen," she said, as we ran through a heap of used sparklers, "you probably hadn't noticed or anything, but Lisa and Michelle and Jenny aren't talking to me."

We stopped at a corner to let cars go by. "Yeah, well," I told her, "I did know you weren't with them a whole lot yesterday." I wasn't sure what else to say, so I just asked her what I wanted to know. "*Why* aren't they talking to you?"

"It's so dumb." She shook her head. "You know when I lost that contest? Well, afterward I told Lisa how much she'd looked like a coiled-up rattlesnake on the stage, and she told the other girls, and they sided with her, and they haven't talked to me since, which isn't fair. But I don't think it's *normal* to curl yourself up into circles and roll around like a tire in front of people, do you?"

"I don't know." I puffed as I ran. "I thought she was pretty good. I also think it was mean, what you said to her."

She stopped running. "Mean? *They're* the ones who are mean."

I stopped running too. "What do you mean, mean?" I asked her.

"They're not *talking* to me," she explained. "They're pretending I'm invisible. They're giving me the silent treatment. My grandmother wants to call and tell their mothers on them, but I won't let her. They can't keep it up much longer."

"Remember Marilyn in third grade?" I asked. "You didn't talk to Marilyn for months and months, and when she cried you all laughed."

"That was different." She started running ahead of me. Only a block and a half to go. "I'm pretty sure it was different. Besides, my grandmother thinks Lisa's father knew the contest judges and that's why Lisa won. My grandmother saw him talking to them afterward. And laughing. And shaking hands."

"Maybe he was just saying thank you."

"Maybe. Maybe not."

Toby came barreling down the sidewalk on his Big Wheel, making motorcycle sounds with his mouth. *BR-rrr-BR-rrrrrr.*

"The girls never did this to me before," Molly said. "They'll come back. I know they will. I bet Lisa will roll herself around the stage Sunday at the state contest and get herself a big fat zero score. And then Jenny and Michelle will come back to me again."

We jumped away from Toby's three-wheel attack and ran into the Rossis' front yard, where Molly dumped all the junk onto the grass. Toby spun around and ran over the whole mound of it with his noisy motorcycle.

"Hey, cut that out!" I yelled, but he hadn't broken much. He'd missed the sunglasses and the

Gumby watch with the broken band. Mostly he'd run over the head of a fuzzy pink bear and caught the yellow flannel baby blanket in his big front wheel. The nail clipper wasn't hurt. Neither were the car keys on a pink-elephant key chain, the cassette, the blue heart earring, the two Go Bots that went from robot to jet and back, or the $4.87 in change.

"OK," Molly said, "now what do we do with it?" We sat down on the grass and looked at the pile.

"Where'd you get that stuff?" Toby asked, grabbing for the Go Bots.

"We found it." I grabbed faster than he did and put them back in the bag.

"You going to keep it?" he asked.

"Finders keepers," Molly said, but she didn't sound too thrilled.

"I know what," I told her. "I can advertise all this stuff in the Lost and Found column of the newspaper. It's free when you advertise that you've found something. At the *News-Advertiser* it is, anyway." It's true. Once when this cat followed me home, my mom sent me to the newspaper to put in a free ad. The cat's name, it turned out, was Roscoe, and it lived about two blocks from us. It hissed at my cat, Fido, a lot and tore one of his ears. I was just as glad when the owner came and took it away.

I got paper and some pencils from Mrs. Rossi and brought them out on the grass. While I tried to teach Toby that a nickel and two pennies made seven cents, not three, Molly made a list of the stuff people might want back, except for the money, which nobody could prove was theirs. I thought it was dumb to put the nail clipper on the list, but Molly said what if it was an old family heirloom.

"And then there's this," she said, picking up the little lunch bag. "I don't *care* if somebody wants this back. It's mine. I'm going to wrap it with birthday-present paper so we can take it with us when we go to the ceremony Wednesday. You want to see what's in it?"

Toby had grabbed the Go Bots out of the bag and was trying to twist their little heads off.

"Listen, Molly," I told her, "I can't put something in that capsule with you. I can't even go to the ceremony with you. I've already been seen with you once too often. Like yesterday eating pie. And afterward."

"What's wrong with me?"

"Nothing. Well, something. You're a girl."

"So?"

"Well, you know. I mean, Nick and all those

guys would tease me so much I'd *wish* they weren't talking to me."

She shrugged. I couldn't believe she didn't know what I was talking about. When we were in Mr. Star's room, she and Lisa had to give each other cootie shots practically every time I stepped on their toes or shoved their chairs. Of course now she and Lisa weren't even talking to each other.

"What about cooties?" I asked her.

"That's baby stuff. That's fourth grade. You're not all that bad. Anyway, I'm tired of doing stuff by myself. And I'm sure not going to call the girls and beg." She crossed her arms and looked me in the eye. "You got anybody else to do things with this summer?" she asked.

"Sure. There's . . . well, Toby. And in a few weeks . . . like three weeks . . . Nick. And . . ."

"Three weeks. Right."

"*You* know the kids at school would laugh."

"What do you care? I thought you liked being weird."

I shrugged. That was, of course, true.

"Then you'd rather spend your summer by yourself?"

"Yes," I told her, even though it wasn't exactly true. But still, she *was* a girl. And she *had* kissed me. What if that really did make her my girlfriend?

"All right for you!" she said. She picked up the list and all the things we'd found. "I'm taking these to the newspaper office. But first . . ." She reached into the grocery sack and pulled out the little lunch bag, and out of the lunch bag she took a small can. Holding it out to me, she asked, "You want some candy?"

It was a can of peanut brittle, a kind of ratty-looking can of peanut brittle. It didn't seem to me like such a great idea to eat candy out of a can that you've just found in the garbage, and I told her so.

"Try it," she said. "It's terrific. Didn't kill me."

"I'll try it," Toby told her. "Give it."

"No, this is for Hobie." And she handed it to me.

"I don't much like peanut brittle," I said.

"Try it," she told me.

"Is *this* what you want them to bury? No kidding! Listen, don't you remember from school that if you put stuff like this in the dark it's going to grow tons of disgusting mold? They'll never let you put it in. Never."

"Try it," she said.

I pried the plastic lid off the top, expecting my nose to fill with the sweet, sticky, nutty smell of peanut brittle. But it didn't. That wasn't what it was filled with at all. Instead, while Molly and

136

Toby practically fell apart laughing, a big, fat, springy wire snake all covered with gray-brown cloth whopped out and hit me splat in the face.

And that was what Molly wanted to plant in the time capsule, so those guys in the future would know what we were really like! A spring snake.

I rubbed my nose. "Molly Bosco," I said, "you're weird."

She just smiled.

# 12

# And to Top It All Off...

It rained like crazy on Wednesday, Time Capsule
Day. As I sloshed down the street toward City Hall,
the drops that hit my yellow raincoat sounded like
corn popping. I'd worn my raincoat because I didn't
want to turn into Mud Man while they buried our
interviews and bags of other stuff for people to dig
up after we were dead.

Mrs. Rossi had given me the whole half day off.
Mom had made me wear my new blue birthday
shirt. Dad had told me he was proud of me, but I
knew it was no big deal.

As I slogged down the puddled sidewalk, Toby
waved from his porch and started singing, to show
me how much I'd taught him, "ABCDHI—U."
Catchy tune. If this rain keeps up, I thought, that
time capsule is going to get sucked straight down
through the mud to the center of the earth, and
they'll never find it. Unless, just unless, I decided,
they've set up a big striped tent outside for everybody to stand under. That way the envelopes and
smelly stickers and people will all stay dry.

But when I got to City Hall and its sudsless fountain, I didn't see a striped tent. I didn't see a hole either. All I saw was rain, so I went inside.

Molly was there, drying off a big blue umbrella that was shaped like a Cubs cap with a big bill on it. A few other people were gathered around, making pools on the marble floor. Some of them were adults, some of them kids from other schools. I didn't know anybody but Molly. A sign told us the ceremony would be upstairs in the auditorium, so the line of people in wet raincoats moved up the steps, a waterfall going the wrong direction.

"Where you sitting?" I asked Molly.

"I don't know. Where're you?"

"I don't know, but if you're going to put in the candy can, you better sit up front," I told her.

She sat in the front row and I sat behind her. It took a while for the auditorium to get full, so we talked to kids around us, asking them what they were burying. One junior-high boy was putting in a yearbook autographed to The Children of the Future. A junior-high girl was giving them her last-year's gym suit. This one girl had a tape of her class singing their end-of-the-year concert. A guy whose shoes had mud up to the tongues had walked all the way around City Hall looking for the time hole. He said he thought maybe they'd decided to shoot the capsule into space instead. When people asked Molly what she was adding, she just looked mysterious and said it was a surprise.

"Ladies and gentlemen, boys and girls!" the mayor said into the microphone. She looked a whole lot different from when she climbed out of the dunk tank. Drier, for one thing. She smiled a lot until everybody got quiet, and then she talked a lot about the past and the present and the future and how we were little cogs in big wheels, and only part of the big picture, and tiny grains of sand on the vast beach of time.

Then a serious-looking man from the Jaycees told us we should step forward when he called our names. I poked Molly in the back of the neck to let her know that nobody was going to call her name. He went on to say he'd give us the stuff the school or organization we represented had sent in, and each of us should say a few words about what we were contributing.

"You'll have to lie," I whispered to Molly, but she just cocked her head to the side. I couldn't see her face.

I hadn't counted on the "few words" part, and was trying to think of a very few that wouldn't sound dumb when two men in suits came through the door. They were carrying a box, which they put on a table in front of the mayor. The box wasn't cardboard, I'll give them that. It was wood, painted red, and on the side somebody had stenciled STOCKTON, ILLINOIS, TIME CAPSULE, and the date. It was about the size of our school's lost-and-found box, a little bigger than an orange crate, and it sure didn't look waterproof. Everybody stared at it without saying, "Oh, wow, neat," because it wasn't.

Right away I stopped worrying about what those people in the future would think about me liking cereal, the color gray, Molly Bosco, and Mondays. I leaned forward. "As soon as they plant that thing in the ground," I told Molly, "it's going to fill up with water, and the ink on our stories will smoosh right into that junior-high kid's white gym shorts."

Molly turned around, nodded her head like she couldn't agree with me more, and gave a major frown.

All along, people had been trailing in late because of the rain, but this time when the auditorium door opened, the late person was Mrs. Glass. She came hurrying in, her two kids in front of her. She looked around for seats, spotted Molly and me, and waved a folded newspaper at us before settling down.

After the Jaycee guy had called off a couple of people's names, I knew I wouldn't have to give a speech. The first kid who dropped in his envelope said, "This is the stuff from Romona School." Not even the adults sounded like they were giving the

Gettysburg Address. But everybody kept their faces straight at least. None of them knew this was going to end up with a big snake laugh. If Molly dared.

The kid whose name was called just before mine was Chuckie Glass. He dropped in the collage from Mr. Kemp's kindergarten. He didn't say anything.

"Four B at Central School interviewed each other," I told the people, after the guy handed me my envelope. It smelled like a pink, sugar-coated dough-nut. "If those kids in the future are supposed to do reports on this, they shouldn't believe everything we said. Besides, things are already a lot different from the way we wrote them in June. Anyway, here it is." The grown-ups clapped like I'd said some-thing smart, and I dropped the 4B envelope into the box, which wasn't even lined with Saran Wrap.

The Historical Society put in some pictures and maps. Someone from the Community Church added their address book. And on and on. It takes a lot of paper to fill a box that big.

"Your turn next," I whispered to Molly, poking her shoulder.

She turned around. "You think it'll be safe in there?"

I shrugged.

"You think they'll let me?"

"Sure," I told her, but I lied.

She stood up, or almost up, just as the Jaycee

guy said, "And finally, to top it all off, here is our very own Robert Cooper, editor-in-chief of the Stockton *News-Advertiser,* to present the last two issues of his award-winning newspaper. Mr. Cooper."

Molly sat down. Mr. Cooper stepped right up. He was waving last week's newspaper. It had a picture covering the whole first page. The paper always has a big picture on the front. This one was of a guy who'd just been elected president of the Board of Education. He had on a bow tie. Mr. Cooper pointed to the guy and talked about the schools of the future.

I was getting bored, so I kicked the back of Molly's chair. She unwrapped the top of the can, turned around, and pointed the plastic cap at me like she was going to shoot it off. I reached over and shoved her umbrella on the floor. "Shhhhhhhhh," somebody said.

Mr. Cooper kept right on going. ". . . and to-day's paper is just chock-full of pictures showing our glorious Fourth of July celebration. Here it is, hot off the press, to let those folks of the future know with what joy and excitement, with what pure pleasure, we remembered our forefathers and the founding of our nation."

Mr. Cooper had the paper open to the middle, pointing at pictures of fireworks and pony riders. I wondered if those future people would have sparklers and bingo games and not think a lot about us or George Washington. I didn't think about forefathers even once on the Fourth of July.

"That's the paper with our ad in it," I told Molly, and she nodded. "We'll have to get a copy when the program's over."

"And this cover shot should really get them going," Mr. Cooper said with a big chuckle, shutting the paper and holding it up for everyone to see.

When Molly saw it she yelped. Then she slunk down in her chair so far, the top of her head disappeared. I froze, like I'd been zapped. The kids around us giggled. The grown-ups looked at the picture and *chuckled*. They chuckled like it was *so* cute.

On the front of the Stockton *News-Advertiser* were two faces, almost as big as life, completely sloshed with whipped cream and toasted coconut. The boy's face was smiling like a toothpaste ad. The girl was kissing the boy on the cheek.

Molly and I had given them a laugh all right, but not exactly the big snake laugh I'd been expecting. It was worse than disgusting. It was *public,* like everybody in the world could point at me. I thought I would die.

# 13

# Future Shock

"Don't they look ridiculous!" the kid next to me said, rolling her eyes. I thought for a minute about crawling under my chair, but then, suddenly, I could tell by the way the kid was laughing that she didn't know it was me she was laughing at. I stared again at the picture. Those pie masks were as good as Halloween.

"Yeah, gross," I said. Then I leaned over and told the top of Molly's head that you couldn't tell who the kids in the paper were.

She straightened up, took a better look, and then started laughing like everybody else. So did I, except maybe a little louder.

In the middle of the big ha-ha, the auditorium door swung open again. Lisa, Michelle, and Jenny stood there all in a row. They were wearing matching green shorts, shirts, hair clips, and plastic shoes.

Molly caught her breath. Then she turned around in her chair and whispered, not quite soft enough, "Don't they look like three lime gummy worms?"

Kids around us giggled. It felt good to hear them laughing at somebody else.

Michelle and Jenny tried to hide from all the eyes, but Lisa walked right in. "Oh, are we late?" she asked, grandly. "My mother thought, like, it would be a lovely gesture if I, like, gave a copy of my certificate to the time capsule." Her curls hopped up and down.

Nobody said anything. Michelle and Jenny moved behind her. "We stopped at the library and made a photocopy of it," she went on. "It's my Official State of Illinois Miss **Pre-Teen** Personality Contest certificate. I won it **Sunday** afternoon over lots of other girls, so I'll be going to Los Angeles in August. It's, like, to show I've got more pre-teen personality than anybody in the state." I kind of hoped she'd do a backward flip or two, but she didn't.

The crowd clapped. Jenny and Michelle clapped. So did Lisa. Molly did not. She'd been wrong about Lisa scoring zero.

"Well, you come right over here, Little Miss Personality," the Jaycee said. He wasn't going to turn down a winner.

Lisa gave the red box a funny look, but she placed her certificate copy in it anyway. Slowly and carefully. She smiled at me, but her eyes slid right past

Molly. Unless something big happened, it looked like Molly wasn't going to be Boss of the fifth-grade girls.

Molly turned around. "I've decided," she told me, "to keep the candy can for something better."

"*Shush,*" somebody said.

After patting Lisa on the head, Mr. Cooper dropped his two award-winning papers in the box, beaming at a photographer who was clicking pictures. He was the same one who'd told Molly to give me a kiss. "Face a little more to the right," he told the Jaycee guy, who snapped the hinged lid shut and turned a little key in the front lock.

"Now," the mayor announced, "it's time for the grand March of Time to the place where our capsule will rest, waiting to be opened on this very date, July tenth, in the year 2091, the two hundredth anniversary of the founding of our fair town." She nodded to a Cub Scout, who blew a toot or two on his bugle. Everybody stood up and followed a batch of Cubs carrying flags that wobbled. It was very official. We marched almost in step out of the auditorium and down the stairs. For the first time, I felt historical.

Yeah, I thought, this is perfect. I should have thought of this myself. We're going to file down some spooky back steps into the dark, moldy basement of City Hall, where there's a single light bulb hanging on a long cord and a hole already dug for this box to live in for eons and eons, with a picture of me in it being kissed by this girl, but nobody will know it's me. We never told that photographer our names. I felt terrific.

Mrs. Glass almost caught up with us as we headed down a dead-end corridor that was lined with office doors. She had the newspaper with her, and I realized that she could tell everybody who was on that cover. And that she probably wouldn't even know we didn't want her to. I hurried on ahead, ducking around the green Lisa triplets, and then I remembered that *they* knew, too.

"Oh, Hobie and Molly, I have something to show you," Mrs. Glass called out. The hall was getting packed with all those time-capsule people. There was no right way to go. Molly turned one way. I turned the other. Mrs. Glass raised her voice. "I wrote a letter to the editor about you."

"About *me?*" the mayor asked. I guess people were always writing letters to the editor about her.

"Oh, no," Mrs. Glass said, and by then everybody was listening. She seemed to like that. "I wrote a letter"—and she held up the paper that had our faces on the front—"about the two lovely children standing in front of you." All those people staring. My stomach ached. I wondered if I could slip into one of the offices or if maybe there was some room left in the red box.

The mayor looked down at me, but I ducked my head and edged behind one of the flag-bearing Cub Scouts. I shook my head at Mrs. Glass, but she wasn't looking. Lisa was.

" 'Dear Editor,' " Mrs. Glass read grandly from the newspaper in her hand. " 'On the Fourth of July, two splendid fifth graders' "—her eyes left the page to search for us; I ducked again—" 'Hobie Hanson and Molly Bosco, won the pie-eating contest for their age group.' " The Green Three were laughing behind me, but Mrs. Glass read on. " 'They also found two treasures—a diamond pin that once belonged to my great-grandmother, *and* my son Chuckie, who was lost in the crowd after the fireworks. I want to publicly congratulate them and thank them for their help.' " She handed the paper to Alex and lifted Chuckie up high, even though he was getting a little big for that. "Those two children are world-class finders, and that's why I wrote a letter to the editor to thank them publicly. And I'm glad that you're preserving it, so the story of their heroism will live for years and years."

"Pie-face heroes," I heard Lisa say. Two laughs echoed hers.

A few adults said stuff like, "How lovely." Molly and I kept moving farther apart.

"Does that mean the kid with the pie on his face was you?" the girl who'd been sitting next to me asked, giggling.

I shook my head and pointed to the Cub Scout in front of me, who looked like he was about six years old.

"Which ones *are* they?" some kid asked. I looked all around like I was searching faces, too.

"Would those two nice children step forward?" the mayor asked. "I didn't realize the cover children were actually here."

Stepping forward was the last thing I wanted to do. I thought about closing my eyes and pretending that I'd disappeared. I thought about saying it wasn't true, but with Mrs. Glass beaming like that, nobody would believe me.

I saw someone moving. Molly had stepped up next to the mayor and kind of curtsied to the crowd.

"You think Hobie *likes* her?" I heard Michelle ask.

"Hobie *hates* her," Lisa said firmly. "I can tell."

"Hobie," Mrs. Glass called out, "don't be shy."

I stepped a half step toward the mayor, and people turned to look at me. The three girls were pointing. Everybody knew. My face, I figured, was going to stay red forever.

That's when the head Jaycee raised his voice and said, "Well, that was really a wonderful, moving story, but our time is short this morning, and we have gathered here to place our own little piece of time in a space we've set aside for it." He grabbed the brass knob and swung open the door in front of us.

I was all set to be the first one down the stairs to that basement, when Molly, who'd pushed in front of me, stepped back and said, with a gasp, "I don't believe this! Is it a joke?" She turned around, shook her head, and called out so all the people in the back could hear, "This isn't a time capsule at all. It's a *broom* closet!"

And that's what it was.

There must have been fifty people in the hall— lime triplets, Cubs, Mrs. Glass and her boys, kids from schools, people from clubs and places—all of us staring into an empty closet. It was empty except for a small brush hanging on a back hook. The grown-ups didn't seem the least bit surprised. Maybe they all thought time capsules were supposed to look like that. The kids, though, knew better.

"My teacher, Mr. Star, told us you were going to *bury* all this," Lisa said, sticking out her bottom lip.

The Jaycee looked pained, like somebody had stepped on his toe.

"Uh, one word of explanation here," the mayor announced, waving her arm, taking charge. She cleared her throat. "We, uh, *had* originally planned to actually, uh, *bury* the time capsule, but short of sinking it in concrete . . ." She smiled broadly and waited for people to laugh. The grown-ups did. "Short of sinking it in concrete, we couldn't think of any possible way to save our precious papers from molding and rotting in the ground. So we, uh, decided to put everything in this small, uh, room, instead, where it will remain nice and dry and safe from the, uh, ravages of time."

The two Jaycees who had carried the red box down pushed it into the closet. It pretty much filled the space at the bottom, but there was still lots of room at the top to hang coats in. Or more brooms, maybe.

"How will they know when to open the door?" a kid asked.

"There'll be a sign." The mayor shook her head. "We're having one made to go right on the front of the door, but unfortunately the painter hadn't finished it by this morning. It will tell exactly when the capsule should be opened."

" 'Do not open this broom closet until July tenth, 2091,' " Molly whispered.

"Or the tooth fairy will fall asleep for a thousand

years," I told her, "and everybody will have to go through life with two sets of teeth."

The mayor turned a regular-looking key in the regular-looking lock. Then she raised the key high in the air for everyone to see, the Cub Scout played his bugle again, and the photographer took about ten more pictures. All the grown-ups clapped. And that was that.

As the people around us hurried away down the long hall, Mrs. Glass and her boys drew up next to us. She handed Molly the newspaper. "This isn't much of a thanks, but there it is." She looked very pleased.

"Thank you," Molly told her.

"Yeah," I said, "thanks a lot."

"And so, what are you two doing with the rest of the summer?" she asked.

"Hi, *Hobie*." Lisa and her shadows were passing by. "I liked your picture." All three of them laughed. "It's so cute, we'll have to show it to *everybody*."

"Oh, Hobie and I have several things we plan to do," Molly said to Mrs. Glass, not once looking at the girls. She held up the candy can, still mostly wrapped with birthday paper. "See this?"

The three girls hung back to listen, and Molly lowered her voice so they had to move in close to hear.

"What's in this package is awesome. really awe- some. And Hobie and I are going to put it in *our* time capsule. Our very own time capsule. Right, Hobie?"

First I'd heard of it. Everybody was kind of star- ing at me. I started to shake my head. No way. Then I looked over at Lisa, who was all set to laugh when I told Molly she'd gone bananas.

"Right, Hobie?" Molly asked again, shaking the can a little.

Our own time capsule with a spring snake in it? Mine? And Molly's? It really didn't sound like a bad idea. Besides, now everybody and the mayor knew it was me with Molly on the cover of the *News-Advertiser,* so what did I have to lose?

I swallowed the "No way." "Right," I said. "And we're going to *bury* our time capsule. In the ground."

"Like *they* were supposed to," Michelle said, looking over at the shut door. "What's in there?" she asked Molly, pointing to the candy can.

"Michelle!" Lisa took a deep, shocked breath. *"Shhhhhh!"* She tugged at Michelle's green shirt. Michelle had broken Rule One, actually the only rule in the silent treatment. She had talked to Molly.

Molly talked back. "I'm afraid it's a secret." She smiled at Michelle. "But we're looking for more things, if you have any. Good things . . ." Her smile turned sly. ". . . Like Lisa's smelly stickers, and, you know, other weird stuff."

Lisa didn't bite. "Come *on*," she ordered the girls, and started to walk away.

"That sounds terrific," Mrs. Glass said. "Don't you think so, boys?" The boys thought so.

The girls, though, were edging toward Lisa.

"We'll give directions so people will know where to find it," Molly went on. The girls had stopped now, listening.

"Like a treasure hunt," I added.

"Can we put something in the capsule?" Alex asked.

"Besides a dumb collage?" Chuckie said.

"Sure," Molly told him. "We'll let a few other special people put things in it." She smiled at the girls.

"A dinosaur?" Chuckie asked.

"If it's small enough," I said.

"This big," Chuckie told me, holding up his thumb.

"Oh, the dwarf variety. For sure," Molly said. Jenny laughed.

"Jenny! Remember what we said," Lisa warned. Pressing her lips together tight, she hurried toward the steps. "I won, you know," she called back to them.

The girls looked after Lisa, then at Molly, then at each other.

"How are you going to let people know when to dig it up?" Alex asked. "Will you put up a sign like they're going to do here?"

Molly bit her lip. Since she was making it up as she went along, she didn't have an answer ready. The girls looked away, and they started to follow Lisa down the steps.

"We'll advertise," I announced. "Put an ad in the paper on the day . . ."

"I'm going," Lisa called.

The girls followed, but they were giggling to each other.

" 'Bye," Michelle called back.

Jenny waved.

"Well, we'll be off, too," Mrs. Glass said. "Let us know when you want to bury the dinosaur. We deliver."

Before they left, though, Alex leaned over to me and whispered something that would have changed practically my whole summer if only he'd said it on the Fourth of July. "I had some coconut yesterday," he told me, "and I liked it."

# 14

# Up, Up, and Away

The hole was about a foot and a half square. My hands had fat blisters on them from all the digging. It was a week after the door had slammed shut on the official capsule. We were just about ready to bury the real one in my hole, which was halfway between two maple trees, right next to the fence in my backyard. It wasn't a bad hole—a little lopsided, but not bad to look at. There were a few worms in it, so I sang, " 'The worms crawl in, the worms crawl out, The worms play pinochle on your snout.' "

"Hobie," Molly told me, "that's not weird. That's gross. There's a difference." She was patting the dirt into a mountain ridge around the hole, so it would look neat for our capsule ceremony.

"Did your daddy say you could do this?" Toby asked me.

"My dad *liked* the idea," I told him. "He said it was just the kind of thing he wanted me to do this summer."

"Bury things?" Molly asked. "You're kidding. Is he weird too?"

I laughed. "He's taking Mom and me back-packing and houseboating down the Illinois River next week. That's pretty weird."

"Somebody's coming!" Toby yelled. "Has the party started?"

"Right now it's starting," I told him. "This minute. Do you know for sure who'll be here?" I asked Molly.

"No. I reached a few kids and left messages for some others. We'll see."

"We're early. I'm sorry," Mrs. Glass said, as she and the boys walked through to the backyard, "but Chuckie couldn't wait."

"Where's the time capsule?" Alex asked.

"Here," I told him, pointing to the yellow baby blanket on the ground, the one left over from the Fourth of July. Lots of stuff was heaped up on it, ready for the ceremony. We even had a bag of Oreo cookies we'd bought with found money, so there'd be refreshments.

"I don't see any capsule," he said.

"That's because you don't know what it looks like. It comes in parts. This is the main part." I handed him a coffee can with red tape wrapped around the outside so you wouldn't think we were burying the Hills Brothers. The can wasn't huge, but then we didn't have very much to bury, and besides, I didn't want to dig a bigger hole.

"Can I put my dinosaur in now?" Chuckie asked, holding up a small piece of blue-gray plastic.

"That's a *Tyrannosaurus rex,*" Toby told him. Dinosaurs are his friends.

"I *know* it," Chuckie said, eyeing this other expert.

"His tail is chewed." Toby pointed.

"A brontosaurus did it. A mean brontosaurus." The two of them sat down under one of the maple trees and hid the dinosaur in grass that was taller than its head.

"Hi, Hobie, sold any dead rats on strings lately?" Trevor and Marshall rolled in on their bikes. Each of them had brought his own folded paper stars for the future. Trevor's were covered with Ts and Marshall's with lightning bolts. They looked good.

"How come *Molly* called us to come to this?" Marshall asked me, pushing up a good old snout nose to let me know what he thought about her.

I shrugged. "Because she said she would. A lot of kids weren't home."

Next came Jenny and Michelle, and—lagging behind like she didn't want people to think she wanted to be there—Lisa.

"I already put my Miss Pre-Teen Personality certificate in the *real* capsule. I don't see what's so big deal about Hobie's," Lisa told Mrs. Glass. "I think this is silly."

"I guess everybody's here now," Molly announced, "so we can start."

I cleared my throat. "Ladies and gentlemen," I said, because that's the way real speeches begin. "Yesterday Molly Bosco and I put an ad in the Stockton *News-Advertiser*. Actually, the guy who wrote the ad down thought we were strange, and he wasn't going to take it at first, because we told him it was an ad we want to run in July of the year 2013."

All the kids looked at each other like they thought we were pretty strange too.

"Anyway," I went on, "Molly wouldn't let him say no, so finally the guy called somebody up on the phone and asked them if it was all right to take our ad, and whoever it was said sure, but they couldn't charge us now because they didn't know what it would cost then. You see what I mean?"

"OK," Marshall said, "I'll bite. What's the ad got to do with that pile of junk on the yellow baby blanket?"

"It's an ad," Molly explained, "that tells people they should open *our* time capsule on July Fourth in the year 2013, and gives directions on how they can find it in Hobie's backyard."

"Why 2013?" Trevor asked.

"I don't know. It just sounds good," Molly told him.

"Well, yeah, there's that, and also we want to be there to watch when they open it and find the stuff." I picked up the coffee-can capsule, snapped the lid off, and held it out. "OK, it's time to begin. Chuckie, you're first."

Chuckie clenched his hand behind him, stepped back, and scowled at us. But then—because everybody was looking, I guess—he leaned forward and dropped in the slightly mauled dinosaur. "Plop, you're dead," he said as it hit bottom.

"Toby, you got yours?" Toby didn't much want to put his in either, but since this other kid had, he stuck his hand in his pocket and pulled out one of the Go Bots we'd found. It had a loose head. He sat it upright, next to the fallen blue-gray beast.

Trevor and Marshall tossed in their paper stars, each one missing on the first throw. Jenny put in a green butterfly hairclip. Michelle, who had at least fifteen lime-green stretchy plastic bracelets on her arm, rolled one off into the can.

Then, I decided, it was my turn. First I put in a pair of slightly used glow-in-the-dark shoelaces, then a pen that writes metallic orange, and a cracked yellow mug that had QUACK written on it. People always like digging up pieces of old pottery.

Finally, I added my own personal favorite. From

the bottom of my dresser drawer I'd brought out my old blue plastic soap box. I opened the lid to show the group what was packed inside. They gasped and gagged and aarged a little, which is what I expected those future people to do. In the box, stuck in Silly Putty, was my almost-complete set of baby teeth. I put the lid back on and wrapped it about ten times with tape.

"That," Mrs. Glass said, "is amazing. Truly amazing."

"There's room for only one more thing, but it's probably the best of all," I said, and Molly stepped forward.

"It's that package she had at City Hall," Jenny told the other girls.

"What's she got?" Lisa asked me.

"Oh, it's just this stuff I found in the park after the Fourth of July," Molly told her.

"Well, what's in it that's supposed to be so, like, great?" Lisa asked me. "It doesn't look very awesome to me."

"We're going to let those future people open it and find out," I told her.

"It looks like candy. If it is, it'll go moldy and poison by then, and it will, like, kill them, and then it'll be all your fault. All Molly's fault." Lisa looked pleased.

"You really want to see?" I asked her.

"Of course not," she said. "I just wondered. Actually, I could care less."

I took the can from Molly, unwrapped it, and held it out to Lisa. "No kidding. If you want to look that's OK."

She shrugged, but grabbed the can anyway, shook it, and then slowly peeled open the top. The snake, coiled up inside, all set to spring, felt the cap go and leaped out like it was jet powered, swatting her ear as it flew past into the grass. Everybody laughed but Lisa.

She heaved the peanut-brittle can across the yard. "That," she said, "was mean." And maybe it was. But it was just a joke. Even Mrs. Glass had giggled.

"We thought," Molly said, "that except, maybe, for the person who opened it, the people in the year 2013 would think that was very funny. Everybody would think *we* were funny."

"Everybody will think you're sick," Lisa said, talking to Molly for the first time. "I am going to go home and practice for my big contest. I've got better things to do than bury stupid jokes. I've got my career to think about!"

"Don't be like that," Molly told her. "We didn't hurt you. We've got Oreo cookies."

"Cookies make you fat," Lisa said, and she left, turning around only once to see if the girls were following. "You coming?" she asked them.

They hung back, standing next to Mrs. Glass.

"After it's over," Michelle called. "We want to watch."

"Well, hurry up," Lisa said, and walked briskly down the sidewalk. Jenny sighed.

Molly ran for the tossed can, stuffed the snake back into place, and packed the whole thing firmly into the capsule, which we wrapped around and around and around with more red tape. Then we put that into an old cracker tin and two black plastic garbage bags. Inside the last bag, before I pressed out all the air and tied the knot, I added a sign. I'd made it on poster board using permanent Magic Marker and then gotten it laminated at the library so it wouldn't leak. It read, "Beware. If anybody opens this time capsule before July 4, 2013, their ears will turn to prunes, their noses to dill pickles, their eyes to little peeled onions, and their belly buttons to Gob Stoppers. This is no lie, so beware."

"Hobie Hanson," Molly said, "you're weird." And with that she placed the capsule in the hole. Everybody threw in some dirt. We took turns jumping up and down on the mound to make it flat.

"I hope they can follow the directions in the ad," I said. "The capsule is pretty much exactly halfway between the two trees. I sure would hate to see my teeth buried forever."

We ate all but one of the Oreos. Then the Mar-Vor Marvels left with the Glasses. They'd given Mrs. Glass a leaflet, and she'd hired them to mow her lawn.

"I guess we've got to go now," Michelle told me.

"Yeah, we promised Lisa we'd watch her practice," Jenny said. "She's learning a triple backflip for the finale."

"So we've got to go," Michelle said again, but they hung around anyway.

"You staying here with *him?*" Jenny asked Molly. You could hear the cooties in her voice.

"Right," Molly told her. "We haven't planted grass seed on the dirt yet."

Toby and I went into the garage and got handfuls of seed from a sack. When we brought them back and emptied them onto the dirt pile, the girls were still there talking to Molly, but then they wandered off down the sidewalk.

"Do you know what Michelle said?" Molly asked me.

"No, I don't know what Michelle said, except that she had to go."

"Michelle said," Molly began, digging her heel into the mound of seeded dirt, "Michelle said that she and Jenny think that Lisa is stuck up because she won the contest, and that they are thinking about not talking to her, and talking to me instead."

"Why don't you all just talk to each other?" I asked her. "It doesn't make any sense to me."

She frowned. "Might work," she said, "but I doubt it."

"Hey look, the mailman's here," Toby called, and went running to meet him.

Mr. Marsala has been our mailman forever. He was waving a letter at me as he walked up the front sidewalk. Maybe somebody had answered our ad for the things we'd found in the park. Molly had put in my address so her grandmother wouldn't have all that mail to take care of, but so far nobody had written us, not even about the car keys.

"How you doing, Hobie?" Mr. Marsala asked. "Got one for you. Looks like it's from the kid next door. Where is he? Camp or something?"

I gave him the last Oreo and took the letter. Before opening it, I looked back at the place where the time capsule was buried, right at the fence between Nick's yard and mine, and I knew we should have waited for Nick. He was going to be mad at me for doing something that big without him.

Maybe when he got home—without anybody knowing about it, late at night, at midnight even—he and I could sneak into the backyard and dig the capsule up. I could show him the stuff inside and he could add something weird of his own. Like a rubber mouse on a string. I could just see the look on his face when he got that snake in the nose. I hoped, though, his nose wouldn't turn into a warty green pickle. You never can tell.

"Hey," Toby yelled, stepping on my toes to get my attention. "What's Nick say? Read it to me!"

July 14

Dear Hobie,

Thanks for your letter. It took you long enough. I wish I could have seen Miss Ivanovitch sink Mr. Star in the dunk tank. That must have been a blast.

Who won the pie-eating contest? Did you enter? You and me would have creamed them all. I know it. Your bite is twice as big as it was last year, and I've got enough hair to soak up at least half a pie.

I guess it must be pretty dull there. Did you do *anything* yet to put in your paragraph on "What I Did Last Summer"? Anyway, I'll be home in less than two weeks. The summer has gone faster than I thought it would. I've got it all figured out that you and me can start weeding gardens full-time until school starts. Then we'll probably all get in the same class and it'll be like 4B all over again.

Write me back. I hate mail call without letters.

Nick

P.S.  I'm in the Penguin computer group. That's not as good as the Sharks, but better than the Eels.

P.P.S.  There's a girl here whose name is Kimberly. She's not as bad as most girls.

P.P.P.S.  What's Molly doing besides bossing Lisa around?

P.P.P.P.S.  Get Toby's ball off the roof for him.


"My ball's not *on* the roof," Toby said, and his eyes filled up with water. "Nick's gone, so nobody kicks it there anymore." He stuck his thumb in his mouth and started to suck his fingernail off.

" 'Jingle bells,' " I sang to cheer him up.

" 'Batman smells,' " Molly went on.

" 'Robin laid an egg,' " Toby sang, without taking his thumb out.

" 'The Batmobile lost a wheel.' " I poked him in his middle to make him laugh.

Molly picked up Toby's ball from right next to the time-capsule graveyard. "So Batgirl kicked her leg," she sang. She spun the ball till the yellow stars blurred, then dropped it and really blasted it one. The ball rose high in the air, flew up to the Rossis' roof next door, and settled in a bend of the gutter. Toby was so happy that it was all he could do to shriek and bare his baby fangs.